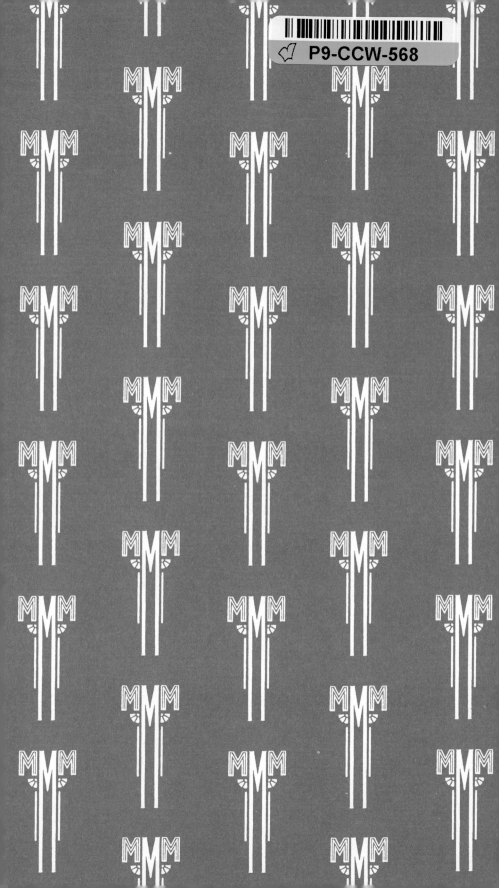

Lost Laysen

MARGARET MITCHELL

Edited by Debra Freer

SCRIBNER

SCRIBNER
1230 Avenue of the Americas
New York, NY 10020

Set in Centaur and Forquet
Designed by Louise Fili and Mary Jane Callister, Louise Fili Ltd

Manufactured in the United States of America

1   3   5   7   9   10   8   6   4   2

Library of Congress Cataloging-in-Publication Data
Mitchell, Margaret, 1900–1949.
Lost Laysen / Margaret Mitchell ; edited by Debra Freer.
p.   cm.
Includes bibliographical references.
I. Freer, Debra. II. Title.
PS3525.I972L67   1996
813'.52—dc20   96-6872
CIP

ISBN 0-684-82428-0

CONTENTS

ACKNOWLEDGMENTS

EBRA FREER WOULD LIKE TO GIVE THANKS AND TO ACKNOWLEDGE THE FOLLOWING PEOPLE AND INSTITUTIONS FOR THEIR ASSISTANCE WITH THIS ENDEAVOR: PATSY WIGGINS, FOUNDER OF THE ROAD TO TARA MUSEUM, without whose inspiration and encouragement none of this would be possible; Henry and Louise Angel Jr., for their memories and fine caretaking of Margaret Mitchell's writings and photos; the Estate of Stephens Mitchell (heir to Margaret Mitchell's writings), for their support of this project and their permission to publish Margaret Mitchell's writings; Courtenay Ross McFadyen and the descendants of Mitchell's other friends—Sarita Hiscox Britton, Dorothy Reeves, Jessie Summers, and Barry Wilkins—for graciously sharing their memories; Mary Ellen Brooks and staff at Hargrett Library and Archives, University of Georgia, for their patience and help; Franklin Garrett and the staff at the Atlanta History Center Archives; Emory University staff at Woodruff Library; Alice McCabe and Bill Baughman, Gwinnett County Historical Society; Wesley Martin, Suwanee Historical Society; staff of Westview Cemetery; staff at the Road to Tara Museum; Susan Moldow; Scott Moyers; Barry Kaplan; Barbara Trimble MacFarlane; Ellen Born; Mary Hopkins Fleming; and my patient friends and family.

N 1916, MARGARET MITCHELL BEGAN WRITING A PASSIONATE
STORY ABOUT A STRONG-WILLED WOMAN WHO PLACES HER
HONOR ABOVE HER LIFE. IT IS A TALE OF UNREQUITED LOVE,
OF A MAN WHO DESIRES THIS WOMAN WITH ALL HIS HEART
but who can never obtain her. He is not Rhett Butler, she is not
Scarlett O'Hara, and this is not *Gone With the Wind.* It is *Lost Laysen,* a
story of love and honor on a South Pacific island, which Margaret
Mitchell wrote in longhand in two blue composition books in the
summer of her sixteenth year.

The tale of *Lost Laysen*'s discovery is itself a bittersweet story of
doomed love and time-honored secrets, of an enduring gift from a
world-renowned writer to a man whom history had almost forgotten.
The man's name was Henry Love Angel. Margaret Mitchell made him
a gift of *Lost Laysen,* and both Mitchell and Angel took the secret of
this remarkable present to their graves.

What makes this present so remarkable? To begin with, Margaret
Mitchell requested that her writings and personal papers be destroyed
after her death. Letters, journals, manuscripts (including most of the
original pages from *Gone With the Wind*); in fact, almost everything that
she ever wrote was systematically incinerated, and for sixty years mil-
lions of her fans have had to resign themselves to the fact that
Margaret Mitchell wrote only one novel. Now, magically, *Lost Laysen*
gives us the opportunity to experience this incomparable storyteller's
gift anew. There will never be another Margaret Mitchell. There will
never be another *Gone With the Wind.* In *Lost Laysen,* we are reminded why.
Through this missing chapter from her life, we can see her spark first

ignite, and anticipate the impending blaze of creativity that would produce *Gone With the Wind*.

When the Road to Tara Museum of Atlanta, Georgia, unveiled Henry Love Angel's legacy in April 1995, the world heard a remarkable kind of rebel yell—another story written by Margaret Mitchell did exist! Telephone calls and media inquiries poured in from around the world. From South Africa to Tokyo to London, people clamored to know more about the discovery. The museum's involvement began in August 1994, when Henry Angel Jr. called for the first time. Angel knew few details about his father's relationship with Margaret Mitchell, but he knew that his father had kept a stack of letters, a couple of her old composition books, and many old photographs.

Henry Jr. was seeking a buyer for his father's keepsakes, but he didn't want them in the hands of a private collector, where the world would never see them and never know the truth about Margaret Mitchell's relationship with his father.

When he died in 1945, Henry Love Angel left behind an untold story in the form of these letters, photos, and two composition books, a secret shared only with Margaret Mitchell and his parents. For more than three-quarters of a century, this untold story, these mementos of Henry and Margaret's affection, silently reposed, first in Henry's parents' home, then in his son's.

It was some time after his grandmother's death in 1952 that Henry Jr. received his father's legacy, carefully saved by her for decades. When his grandfather presented him with his father's secret keepsakes, Henry Jr. was startled: he was aware that his family had known Margaret Mitchell, but he never suspected that his father was an old and dear beau. Still, Henry Angel Jr. recalls that at the time he was given the items, he thought, "What do I want with a bunch of old love letters and photos?" He placed them in a chest of drawers, where they remained, overlooked, for the better part of his lifetime. He almost forgot they were there but was reminded when he heard about an Atlanta museum dedicated to *Gone With the Wind* and Mitchell. He went to a library and looked for his father's name in a Margaret Mitchell biography. There he was, barely mentioned. Henry Jr. decided to contact the museum.

Until Henry Jr. called, Henry Love Angel was little more than a footnote in Mitchell biographies. Biographers make note of him as a passing acquaintance or at best as one of her five known suitors. The museum's president, Patsy Wiggins, believed that if this find was true, and Henry and Margaret Mitchell were closer than anyone had previously realized, then Angel's importance was somehow overlooked. But before agreeing to acquire Angel's keepsakes and learning of their authenticity, the museum approached cautiously. Were Angel's keepsakes worth acquiring? An independent expert was called in, to evaluate the material on behalf of the museum. As a seasoned Mitchell historian, an educated appraiser of fine art and antiques, and a collector for over twenty-five years, I felt prepared for this task. Still, I was astonished to see the abundance of presumably unknown material from this early period. After extensive research, I concluded that these materials were bona fide and a meaningful historical discovery, their importance creating a necessity for portions of Mitchell's life story to be rewritten. The continued study of these items has now revealed a wealth of new information about Margaret Mitchell's life, and additional details will undoubtedly emerge.

The fifty-seven photographs, the fifteen pieces of correspondence, and the story written in two composition books by Mitchell represent the largest cache of unpublished material to surface since Mitchell's death. To appreciate fully the significance of this find, one must recall the indelible mark Margaret Mitchell and her one published novel have left on this country.

Margaret Mitchell's husband John Marsh observed that "what

was written and said [upon Mitchell's death in August of 1949] . . . attested to the unique position she held in public admiration and respect. No other author, and few of any rank, could have been so universally mourned." Indeed, no other single novel has so affected our culture. Published in 1936, it was an instant critical and commercial smash, garnering that year's Pulitzer Prize and spawning the multiple Academy Award–winning movie in 1939. Statistics don't do justice to the extent to which *Gone With the Wind* is a cultural phenomenon, but they help: it has sold more than 30 million copies in twenty-seven languages and continues to sell 250,000 copies worldwide each year. It's said to be the best-selling novel in history. *Gone With the Wind* fans and memorabilia collectors can be found on every continent. The story has blurred historical fact with fiction: for decades since its first publication, visitors have arrived in Atlanta looking for Tara. Now, *Gone With the Wind* does not stand alone.

Margaret Mitchell wrote *Lost Laysen* ten years before she began *Gone With the Wind.* She started writing the story on July 10, 1916, and by August 6 she had finished it, as she recorded on an inside page of her composition book. Pasted in the back of the book is her twelve-chapter outline. The handwritten text is remarkably clean, with few changes or erasures. It's as if the story flowed from her imagination fully formed in slightly less than a month. The fact that a novella of the complexity of *Lost Laysen* was written in so short a span is impressive; that Margaret Mitchell was less than four months from her sixteenth birthday when she wrote it is nothing short of astonishing. *Gone With the Wind* is no fluke.

In a number of fascinating ways, *Lost Laysen* foreshadows *Gone With the Wind.* It contains themes and character types essential to our understanding of the later work. Both works have a love triangle at their center, and both hinge on unfulfilled passion. In both, the heroine is an independent woman who is not afraid to break society's taboos. Other similarities can be mentioned without spoiling the story: *Lost Laysen*'s Billy Duncan, like Gerald O'Hara, is a rough-hewn Irishman with a temper, forced to flee his homeland. Like Scarlett, *Lost Laysen*'s heroine, Courtenay, must cope with a shocking assault, and like Frank Kennedy and Ashley Wilkes, *Lost Laysen*'s Doug Steele and Billy Duncan feel honor bound to pursue the perpetrator. In both works a tremendous cataclysm divides the lives of all concerned. And the ending of neither work lacks for drama.

Also like *Gone With the Wind*, *Lost Laysen* is drawn from Margaret Mitchell's own life. The heroine of *Lost Laysen* is named after Mitchell's best friend, Courtenay Ross. In truth, though, the character, a petite but strong-willed woman, bears a much greater resemblance to Margaret herself, and the hero, Billy Duncan, an honorable, adventurous, rough-around-the-edges man who's willing to fight for his love's honor, strongly resembles Henry Love Angel. In fact, Duncan's relationship with the fictional Courtenay mirrors Angel's to Mitchell: he's a man in love with a woman who returns his affection but ultimately fails to choose him, the devoted suitor mesmerized by a woman he can never win.

Margaret Mitchell's letters and photographs are indispensable to a richer understanding of *Lost Laysen,* and they are included here. They reveal a level of intimacy between Margaret Mitchell and Henry Love Angel so deep, so clearly heartfelt, that they've left Margaret Mitchell scholars dumbfounded. Taken as a whole, they tell a story of love just as magical as *Lost Laysen* itself.

We may never really know the reason that Margaret gave this tale of unfulfilled love to Henry, her unsuccessful suitor. But little wonder that she did, for here was a man filled with such rare devotion to her that, however disappointed, he remained true to his honor, keeping their secret to the end.

(From left to right) Courtenay Ross, Henry Love Angel,
and Margaret Mitchell, circa 1920.

INTRODUCTION

MARGARET MITCHELL AND

HENRY LOVE ANGEL—A LOST LOVE

Besides the novella <u>Lost Laysen</u>, Henry Love Angel's legacy
includes letters, photographs, and negatives. The photos show Margaret
Mitchell ranging in age from eighteen months to the age of twenty-
two. Many of the photos were taken by Henry Love Angel himself;
he enjoyed photography and had a darkroom in the house. His images
of Margaret seem to capture the timeless essence of this remarkable
person, unique and yet part of an emerging new breed of Southern
woman. Mitchell's letters to Angel, touching on the mundane
and the intensely serious, were written between 1920 and 1922.
They are the only surviving chronicle of their love.

ARGARET MUNNERLYN MITCHELL AND HENRY LOVE
ANGEL WERE BOTH BORN IN 1900. THEIR MUTUAL
FRIEND COURTENAY ROSS WAS A YEAR OLDER. THEY
WERE ALL NEWCOMERS TO THE PEACHTREE STREET
area during the 1912–13 school year. Margaret and her family moved
into their new home at 1149 Peachtree Street from across town, and
Henry and Courtenay were both new to Atlanta. Henry Angel was
from Wilmington, North Carolina, and Courtenay Ross was from
Memphis, Tennessee. The three new neighborhood outsiders soon
became close friends, and they were destined to play significant roles
in one another's lives.

There are no letters from Margaret to Henry during the early
period from their youth, and few existing photographs. They were too

Eighteen-month-old Margaret frolics in the yard. "She always scowled as an infant," her brother Stephens once said.

BELOW
Two-year-old Margaret Mitchell almost smiles in this unattributed studio portrait. Both infant photographs were found with Henry Angel's posessions. Perhaps Margaret gave them to him as a jest, in response to a request for a photograph.

busy being children. Margaret was no ordinary child, however; her brother Stephens recalled that she began writing stories as soon as her fingers could guide a pencil and join letters into words.

Between 1912 and 1916, Margaret began to write and produce plays. These productions starred Margaret and her friends, and they were generally staged at the family's new home. Courtenay, Henry, and the rest of the neighborhood gang sometimes filled the ranks as actors. What stirred this creative output? Margaret was undoubtedly influenced by stories about Henry's father, the late actor Henry Waters Angel, and his theatrical exploits. Then, too, this was the age of vaudeville, and the dawning of a new medium, the motion picture.

In December 1915, D. W. Griffith's Civil War story *The Birth of a Nation* opened at Atlanta

theaters, creating a sensation. Courtenay Ross remembers that Margaret Mitchell wrote a play called *The Traitor,* which seems to have been inspired by Griffith's film and by the writings of Thomas Dixon. In one staging, Courtenay played the mustached villain and Margaret played the hero, Steve. Henry saved a photo of Margaret in that role; perhaps it was his favorite.

*Playwright and actress Margaret Mitchell
poses as Steve Hoyle in her play* The Traitor.

Courtenay recalled during a 1980 interview that she and Margaret were like "Siamese twins" during their high school days at Washington Seminary. She went on to say, "We joined a boys' baseball team, I as pitcher, Peg as catcher. A boy named Henry [Love Angel] joined us. He would have been known as a hippie now, so we dubbed ourselves 'The Dirty Three,' 'D.T.' for short." The three played baseball and fought mudball wars together.

In 1916, the D.T. Club had a real war to think about. The Great War

*Courtenay and Margaret
as sophomores at
Washington Seminary
in Atlanta, 1915–16
(bottom row, center
and right).*

cried out from across the Atlantic, and their days of childhood were washed away forever. It was the beginning of the end of innocence, for the world and for these three friends. One can see the contrast in the faces of Margaret and Courtenay between photos taken in their sophomore and junior years. Margaret, Courtenay, and Henry were no longer children.

Margaret began writing *Lost Laysen* on July 10, 1916, the day before Henry's birthday. It would be almost four months before Margaret, too, would turn sixteen years old, yet somehow that summer an extraordinary young woman emerged from the shoes of a child.

Courtenay remembered that she and Margaret were already accepting dates in the summer of 1916. Their social life began to blossom, and as their junior year progressed, they both joined many clubs at school, including the Drama Club, the College Preparatory Club, the First Aid Society, and the Literary Society. November 24 marked the first of many social events for Margaret and Courtenay, a dance given by Courtenay's parents at the Piedmont Driving Club.

Some time that year, an Atlanta boy named Red Upshaw and his family moved away from Atlanta to Raleigh, North Carolina, but he returned for Courtenay's June 1917 party. Red would develop into Henry Love Angel's enemy and later, to the surprise of Margaret's friends, Margaret's first husband.

Despite President Wilson's 1916 campaign slogan that "he kept us out of war," entering World War I was now on the minds of many Americans, and Henry, like other young Atlanta men, was already preparing for battle. In January 1917, Atlanta was selected for a military camp site; by April, the United States had declared war on Germany. In May, a disaster of a sort not seen since General Sherman's March occurred: fire consumed over 300 acres of the city. Ten thousand people were left homeless, and Atlanta was once again under martial law. Margaret and her mother aided and gave comfort to victims of the disaster.

Both Margaret and Courtenay also participated in the Red Cross drive to assist with the war effort. By that fall, Atlanta opened Camp Gordon, another military site; a telephone exchange was added, and Margaret's new number, Hemlock 5628, rapidly became a popular number with many young soldiers.

It was now Margaret and Courtenay's senior year at Washington Seminary. Throughout the year, they attended dances and teas and provided needed distraction for the gallant doughboys. They were again members of the same school clubs, and this year Margaret was president of the Literary Society. The girls' mention in the school's "Senior Class Prophecy" is telling, and it contains a faint but distinct echo of *Lost Laysen*: "Scrambling briskly out over the propeller came none

Courtenay and Margaret in their junior class photo, 1916–17 (bottom row).

Surrounded by an array of summer flowers, a confident Henry Angel (right) displays his bouquet for Margaret; a young Red Upshaw (left) flashes a leering smile. This may have been a group outing, because Margaret later wrote that the last time she saw Red was "out with Courtenay."

BELOW
Henry Angel and Red Upshaw sit on the front porch of Henry's home.

other than Margaret Mitchell. As she threw back her trim aviator's coat I discovered the childlike Buster Brown collar. . . . A submarine was bobbing up and down. . . . In the tower, her eyes riveted to a pair of binoculars, her hand upon the pistol at her belt stood Courtenay Ross. . . . The saucy little boat danced out of my view and in its wake . . . grew a rocky island."

The summer that followed their senior year marked the eve of Margaret's departure for college, and Henry's for war. During this time, Margaret had many beaux, including Henry Love Angel. Henry was an acceptable escort to Margaret's parents, who had watched him grow from a small boy into adulthood and knew his family. Henry's mother was from an old established family that traced its roots back to Benjamin Franklin, and she was also a Baldwin, a respected name in Southern history. The Mitchells may also have thought Henry an enterprising young man; as his son, Henry Jr., recalls, Henry Angel had an aptitude for working on gasoline engines, and would later invent a carburetor design that he would attempt to patent. The Mitchells were equally fond of his old hometown, Wilmington, a seaport on the North

Henry Angel and Margaret Mitchell dressed to the
nines for an unknown special occasion.

Carolina coast that was the main port for Confederate blockade runners and was steeped in history. The Mitchell family frequently took vacations at nearby Wrightsville beach.

Margaret left Atlanta to begin her freshman year at Smith College in Northampton, Massachusetts. Courtenay remained in Atlanta to attend business school. In the fall of 1918, Margaret suffered a heart-rending blow. News reached her that Clifford Henry, one of her beaux, was killed in action in France on October 16. Shortly after, in January 1919, she received even more jolting news. Her mother, Maybelle Mitchell, was dead from Spanish influenza. Margaret returned home to find her father almost overcome with grief. She attempted to return to Smith, but left for good after her freshman year. Margaret seemed to feel that her place was with her father and the care of their family home. It was a decision that she would later find bittersweet.

Margaret and an unidentified friend
show off the latest fashions.

Margaret Mitchell poses with
Henry's camera, her feet dangling
above the running board.

Maybelle Mitchell, cutting flowers
earlier that same day. It is one of the
last photos taken before her death.

*Private Angel poses on
the parade ground.*

During this same period, Henry Love Angel was in the army, stationed south of Atlanta at Camp Benning. He rose quickly through the ranks and was promoted to sergeant in April 1919.

The army was good to Henry and produced in him a confident, virile competitor among Margaret's circle of beaux. Henry would return home on furlough to see Margaret, and he was as much in contention for her affections during this period as anyone else, if not more so.

The war ended in 1918, but Henry's service was not completed until later in 1919. After being honorably discharged, Henry returned to Atlanta. Over the summer of 1919 and for the next two years, Margaret, Henry, and their friends caught the train known as the *Belle* from Atlanta to a place called Shadowbrook Farm located in the rolling countryside of Suwanee, Georgia. Shadowbrook Farm was owned by a family friend, Atlanta attorney Victor Lamar Smith. Smith owned about 800 acres of inherited and acquired land, part of it bordering the Southern Railroad. A ten-foot wooden sign marked the landing of his own private train stop. It was a favorite getaway for Margaret and her friends, who loved to hike, swim, ride horses, and escape from the city. Shadowbrook was the site for many "House Parties" (as they were known), but not for Southern ladies without a chaperone. Among Margaret and her friends, a House Party was a popular occasion that generally involved plenty of fun, food, and socializing. The following images record just such a gathering, some time during late summer. During this time, Margaret began to suspect that Courtenay might elope with her fiancé, Bernice "Mac" McFadyen, but instead, in September, Courtenay entered art school in New York.

Corporal Angel proudly shows off his uniform,
atop Stone Mountain, Georgia.

The proud parents of Henry Angel have now turned the camera to
capture Margaret Mitchell on the arm of their handsome son. It seems
as if Margaret is drawing attention to the ring on her wedding finger.

*Henry and an unidentified comrade
take a break from their jobs in the
Motor Pool Transport Division.*

*The newly decorated Sergeant
Angel, with his mother, Carrie, and
stepfather, D.D. Summey.*

Holding his prized .22 rifle, Henry Angel kneels next to Margaret Mitchell, sitting on the pipe. Seated next to her is Shadowbrook Farm's owner, Victor Smith. Standing behind him (on right) are Courtenay Ross and Mac McFadyen. Behind the fence (from left to right), Henry's friend Skeet, an unidentified chaperone, and Dave Hiscox look on as Courtenay appears to be joking with Dot Havis (in white hat).

LEFT *Margaret Mitchell, Mac McFadyen, and Courtenay Ross (left to right) during a visit to Shadowbrook Farm, photographed by Henry Love Angel.*
RIGHT *Henry, Margaret, and Mac, photographed by Courtenay. Note the jeweled leather gun holster strapped to Henry's leg.*

Mac now wields Henry's camera. Henry and Margaret are arm in arm, while Henry seems to hold a buttercup under Courtenay's chin. Note the ring Margaret wears on her wedding finger; perhaps it is the one that Henry gave her and she later returned.

LEFT *Henry Love Angel and Margaret Mitchell in front of Shadowbrook's farmhouse. An unconfirmed story has it that Margaret and some friends rode their mounts into the small town of Buford, Georgia, in Old West "shoot 'em up style," causing quite a ruckus.* RIGHT *Sporting her riding outfit, Margaret poses for Henry. At this point, she still wears a ring on her left finger.*

Equestrian Margaret Mitchell (center) with friends Courtenay Ross (right) and Helen Turman. A horse can be seen to the left behind Helen.

Friends watch as Margaret Mitchell loads Henry's gun for some target practice. The farm's cornfields can be seen in the distance.

Skeet aims a handgun, while Henry and Dave wait their turn to test their marksmanship. It was not uncommon for average citizens, particularly those returning from the war, to possess a weapon and assay their skill.

The year was 1920, the dawn of the new "anything goes" decade that would become known as the Roaring Twenties, or the Jazz Age. It marked the start of Prohibition, and with it bathtub gin, the speakeasy, the vamp, the flapper, gun-toting gangsters, and bootleggers. Henry Love Angel basked in the light of Margaret's attention. Since he had left the service, he had lived only blocks away from Margaret until late that summer, when he moved out to Shadowbrook. The letters from Margaret that Henry preserved date from this point until her return from her honeymoon in September 1922.

The first letter is from that summer, possibly at the time her foot was in a cast as a result of a swimming accident. It is undated, and was found with no envelope.

Angel, Mon Cher—

Please, if you haven't anything to do, tonight, go out to the Sem. tonight and ask for Dorothy Orr or Mrs. Bob Smith and tell them you are the "barker" I spoke of. Please make it plain to them how I hate not to be able to come and dance but honestly, old dear, as I'm feeling a little better it would be foolish for me to jeopardize my chance of recovery. You will explain how sorry I am, won't you? I know they could shoot my feet, but I can't help it. I ought to go down there this afternoon and see if there is anything I can lend them, in way of pillows, costumes, victrola etc. but I can't go in this rain. You lay it on thick for me—won't you? I'm sorry I couldn't talk to you, this morning, but I know you understand. I don't know when I can call you as I'm trying very hard not to climb the steps. So, I'm writing you instead. I feel great as long as I lie flat so I know you wouldn't ask me to get up.

Henry, do you know if your mother has cut out that chiffon waist I left with her? I've read up everything in the house and sewed up everything too, so I'd just love to have it to sew on, if she's cut it out, it and the little chiffon skirt too. Helen* is coming, so I must stop—This is just to tell you I'm thinking of you.

Peg†

---

*Helen Turman, a friend of Margaret's who had been attending Barnard College, had been pictured in the news at a suffragette rally in New York.
†It was by this point in her life that Margaret Mitchell was calling herself Peg or Peggy, a name she adopted during her college days at Smith. This change in name was significant to her, and Mitchell is referred to as Peggy in this introduction where appropriate, in recognition of that fact.

Henry's love and devotion for Peggy were no secret. Proposing to her had
now become so customary that they had both perfected a sense of humor about it.
In this proposal scene staged for the camera, Peg feigns approval as Henry
slips a ring on her finger. The caption written in a friend's scrapbook reads,
"Angel proposing to Peg for the 1,000th time. Can you guess the answer?"

Mitchell and Henry loved to act out dramas in front of the camera. Here, Peggy and Henry appear to imitate popular stars from the silent-film serial The Perils of Pauline. Here, Scene I of one such performance: Peggy slides down a ravine by the railroad tracks to retrieve her hat.

Scene II: Henry to the rescue.

Scene III: "The Perils of Peggy" has almost reached its happy ending. Fred Hubbell gives a hand to Peggy as Frances Brown looks on.

The "gang" at "House Party #3": Henry and Peggy stand looking over friends (from left to right) Frances Brown, Phyllis Wilkins, Miss Hitchcock (back row), Skeet and Dot Havis (lying on ground), Jimmy Reese (wearing glasses), Ginny Johnson, Harry Hallman, Edythe Davis, and Dave Hiscox. With the exception of Mitchell, a number of the women worked together at the War Office.

PREVIOUS
Peggy Mitchell performs a balancing act with Henry Love Angel on the tracks of the Southern Railroad. Note that Henry has a handkerchief around his head and a handgun in his pocket.

In late summer, Peggy Mitchell, Henry, and their friends assembled at Shadowbrook Farm, a gathering that would come to be known, somewhat infamously, as "House Party #3." During this occasion, Peggy can be seen (above) wearing a pair of stolen boys' trousers; it is said that she provided entertainment for the gang by acting out parts from a story. It was a memorable event, immortalized in many scrapbooks: those in attendance received prints from Henry's negatives. Henry's photographs amply demonstrate how happy the two of them were together.

In August, Peggy Mitchell was traveling on a train bound for

Kanuga Lake, North Carolina, when she wrote two notable letters, placed in one envelope.

9:10 p.m. "En route Hendersonville"

Well, Angel, I'm off, at last—two groaning suitcases, one million golf clubs (not mine I'm taking them up to the girl I'm staying with), a raincoat, a bushel of magazines and my own unimportant little self. W.B. and Court were to come down and see me off, but either I got on before they arrived or else he, "for various reasons," was unable to fill his dates. Do you know I've been sitting here thinking what you all did Sunday night—and just wondering, too, exactly <u>why</u> you went to all that trouble to extract that information from him when you could have asked me and I'd have told you whatever you wanted to know. Furthermore, old dear, I ain't a-tall satisfied with the information you told me that you <u>did</u> extract from him. No—I'm not saying that any-body fibbed, but there's a nigger in the woodpile somewhere. Either you didn't tell me all he said—or he didn't tell you the whole truth—simply because it wasn't "friendly" and it wasn't in his nature to be plain "friendly." Either he's stinging me—or you—or you're holding out on me. Ok! well—it doesn't matter—someday I'll get the straight of it!

Sorry I was so grouchy this afternoon but you know friends have to suffer when other friends act naturally—because it's only around friends you can act naturally. My nerves were about shot and that in itself annoyed me because I do loathe these women who are always having "nerves"—don't you? Then that ornery date kept ragging me about being an "unnecked vamp" and that I'd "never realize what I was missing." I hated him for it but considering the mood I've been in lately you must admit that I had a wee bit on my mind. I'm going to turn in now—so "au 'voir." Be my good boy till I can get back and keep a maternal eye on you and don't get into trouble.

Good night
"old dear"

THE SECOND

11:30 p.m.

I can't sleep, seems as if I'll go crazy lying here in the dark, listening to the click of the wheels—so you must suffer.

A while back, we stopped for a long time at a station, I don't know where. As I rolled over to look out the window, I spied something on the

platform that made me sit up. It was an "over seas" coffin with an American flag draped over it. The station was very still, there was only one light on the platform—directly over the box—no one was near. I sat here in the dark, hugging my knees, thinking of that boy, wondering if he had a sister or a mother or a sweetheart—wondering too, rather *foolishly, if he wasn't just a little lonesome and hurt, that there was no one to meet him or care—after he had come all that long way and given everything. I felt that I knew him, some how and some thing in me began to ache. The train wouldn't go on. I lay on my face and tried to shut out every thing—but the picture was just as vivid—that chap coming home and no one there.*

Oh well, the train's gone on now, as we pulled out, the wind flapped a corner of the flag by way of farewell, I guess and I wanted— oh, so desperately to cry—but somehow I couldn't because after all, I guess that the dead ones are the lucky ones—n'est-ce-pas? I guess if I hadn't been so on edge, it wouldn't have affected me so but things like that will rip the lid off memories I thought I had bottled up forever. Forgive me, my dear, for I must talk to someone or else flirt with the porter (large and yaller). I told you I was morbid and you wouldn't believe me—wish you could see me now. I'm going to indulge in a wild "orgy of memory" now and then like you and Virginia swear off forever. Wish me luck

---

Tune "Alice Blue Gown"
In my sweet little bathing suit when I first slid down the chute-the-chute. I love both land and sky for I caught every eye and shocked all the people who were passing by. Home Sunday or Monday. Get my letter?

Peg.

In late September, Margaret (as she was still referred to in Atlanta society columns) and Courtenay were included in a local newspaper story featuring the debutantes of the 1920 and 1921 social season. However, Courtenay refused to debut, instead announcing her plans to marry Lieutenant "Mac" McFadyen. On October 8, a theater party was given in her honor by the D.T. Club, hosted by Henry Love Angel and friends.

Four days after this party, Henry Angel received Courtenay's official wedding invitation. The service took place at St. Luke's Episcopal Church. This was Henry's church, too. It would also be the faith under the auspices of which Margaret "Peggy" Mitchell, baptized and raised Catholic, would later marry and be buried. Courtenay and Mac were married at high noon on October 21, and Peggy served as maid of honor. The newlyweds then left for their honeymoon in New Orleans and later set sail for Mac's new post in the South Pacific—two locations, perhaps not coincidentally, that loom in Mitchell's fiction.

It was debutante season, and "Margaret" was making her grand entrance. But "Peggy" had had just about enough of being paraded, and she begged Henry to arrange for her and her friend Helen Turman

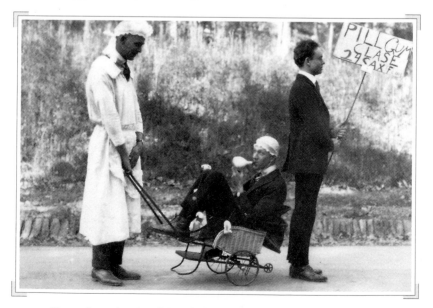

Henry Love Angel and friends ham it up. Henry sits in the carriage.

to visit him at Shadowbrook, in a
letter sent by special delivery and
postmarked February 5, 1921.

Friday p.m.

*Listen, my dear. Helen just called up rarring to go up with me but
wanting to know about chaperones. I had to tell her that I didn't know.
I can't come up till we get "chapped." I never wanted to go any where
so much in my life so please tell Mr. Smith to drag in some rag and
bone and hanker hair for us. If you can get one, my dear, we'll come
up on the 5 A.M. Monday Morning. Could you let me know as soon
as you get this whether we can come? Phone, special, or wire. Naturally
Helen wants to know so she can make her plans for next week in case we
can't come. As for me—please for God's sake, fix it so that I can come.*

*Later (in my room—temperature zero) the phone rang. It was
one of dad's cousins who I had not seen in years. She invited us all to a
family reunion on Thursday. Dad accepted for us so I said I'd be glad
to go and would come back to town for it. You'd have thought that that
would have been all. But he remarked that if I didn't go they would
never forgive me—to which I remarked that that was rather silly. That
started him on one of those—"If that's the way you feel about going"
talks—when I had just remarked that I would love to go!*

*Any way, I'm upstairs in the cold now but I'd rather freeze than
wrangle when there is no cause or gain.*

Please, my dear, see if you can't fix it. I'm pretty tired and a little sick too, and I should love to come up. Give Mr. Smith my love. Tell Skeet not to flirt too hard with any buxom country lasses but to save his flirts till we get there and maybe we'll kiss him if he's a good boy.

Don't get too lonesome, dear boy and take care of your self. Remember that every solid brick you put into a foundation of good health is a brick laid for me and that I appreciate it, even tho' I may not speak of it. Eat beaucoup and sleep beaucoup—exercise "un peu" and clear your mind of all worry—if not for your sake, for mine. If I come up I want to throw aside all my worries and every body else's too. Please help me.

I know this is a very jerky letter but the room is freezing. I am going to bed to keep warm. I'm not exactly up to scratch so a little sleep won't hurt. D. J. sends his best to you and Red wishes you luck. I miss you— "beaucoup."

Let me know with out delay please, if it will be convenient for Mr. Smith to have us up on Monday morning—will you?

's ever—Peg

Margaret danced into the news on March 1, 1921. She and a Georgia Tech student A. S. Weil stunned onlookers at a debutante-sponsored charity ball by performing a wildly suggestive dance that ended with a long kiss. They had perfected the routine by watching it again and again in the film *Four Horsemen of the Apocalypse*. Atlanta dowagers were horrified by the display, and it cost Margaret dearly in these social circles; several months later, she was rejected by Atlanta's Junior League. Ironically, the debutante ball was held at the Georgian Terrace Hotel, where Mitchell delivered her *Gone With the Wind* manuscript to Macmillan editor Harold Latham fourteen years later, and where film stars Clark Gable and Vivien Leigh stayed while in Atlanta for the film's premiere in 1939.

The flamboyant Margaret Mitchell models her
dance costume from the infamous Apache dance that
she performed at the March debutante ball.

Monday A.M.

My dear—

Excuse the paper but it is the only kind in the house. I have been inhumanly busy since you left, which is probably the best thing that could have happened to me. We had so short a time to practice this dance that we have been at it every afternoon and night with about one days exception. It comes off on Tuesday and I will certainly be glad. These nights, after practice, I am so tired that I just can crawl in to bed. I think I'm feeling a little better—certainly, I'm looking better. I don't know any more about V. L. Junior than when you left but I haven't had time to think of it really.

I saw your Mother the other day and she showed me your card. I wish I could have been at the dance. Probably I would have appreciated the "vast difference" very much. Thanks for your card, too.

Do you remember speaking of an "experiment" to someone? Well, please remember, the said "experiment" was only tried once. Do you

understand? I'll tell you more later. Also it didn't appeal to me particularly.

Are you feeling better, dear? I hope you are and I want you to
make every effort to come up to the physical standard you had in the
army. Probably, if the salt mines are still in operation, you don't lack
for something to do. The doc said he was very pleased with your heart—
that it had resumed its normal beat—so don't do anything to strain it.
If I hear of you catching a cold, I will crown you. Yes, really—with a
lead pipe shalt thou be crowned!

I was so proud of you, last time I saw you—proud of your love,
your courage and resignation and most of all your self confidence.
Don't let it drop my dear. I have prayed so hard that you would have
it because without it you can never amount to much. With it and work,
the world lies ahead. If ever you begin to get discouraged and lose confidence in your self—draw on my supply for I believe in you. Just set
your mark and go to it.

Have I been preaching? Forgive me, my dear. I have a funny little
way of moralizing upon occasion, haven't I? Probably it's because I
want you to succeed and be strong and confident.

I am sending the salt mine pictures, and also the others. I can't find
the bathing picture but I'll try to send it later.

Give my love to Skeet and Mr. McCrea and "uncle Victor."—also
to you!

Peg.

P.S. I need a refill

In August, Peggy was hospitalized for adhesions to the intestines.
In a letter Peggy wrote to an old college friend, she reveals more of her
feelings about Henry and her other beaux.

At some point, Henry finally did get his swimsuit picture.

... As to who was in my room at Saint Joseph's [hospital] that memorable night, I grieve to state that none of the five were my family. One was Lt. Jimmy Howat—A.W.O.L. from Camp Benning; No. 2 was "The Angel" [Henry Angel] (I believe I wrote you something about him ages ago—when you accused me of kissing a lot of boys—and I told you that I kissed him when he told me that I helped him give up "likker and wild women."); No. 3 was a little doctor, who was with the British Cavalry during the war—a sardonic little devil; No. 4 was Red Upshaw, ex-Annapolis, ex-U. of Ga. football player—also ex-lover of Court's. I inherited him a year and a half ago; No. 5 was Winston Withers, cattle rancher from Alabama prairie country—also an inheritance.

... No, my folks weren't there because I wasn't supposed to have visitors, as I was pretty sick and full of morphine. I didn't know the boys were going to come to town till they turned up and somehow bribed the nurse to let them in. None of them knew that the others were coming, so it was kind of a surprise party all around.... You see, Jim and Red don't like each other much, but they are drawn together in common enmity to the Angel. The little doc spares no one with his irony except Angel, and Winston, bless him, is everybody's friend. So you see, Al, it was some party!... I'm here to state that I haven't lied to those five men—nor have I misled them in any way. Each knows exactly where he stands with me and where the other four stand, too. If I kiss Red good-bye [when] he goes off for a couple of months, the other four know about it and vice-versa....

I thanked them all for the way they'd helped me and yanked me out of trouble during these last six months. Winston addressed the company as "Fellow sufferers gathered here in a common cause," and asked if I had come any nearer making up my mind. I said no, that I loved 'em all and appreciated what they had done for me but didn't have any intention of marrying any of them.

That didn't seem to worry them much, for they made a motion that I be elected "community fiancée." The motion was seconded and carried and the five kissed me goodnight—to my enjoyment and the intense horror of the nurses.

Now that I'm well, I realize more fully that I couldn't marry any of them. Somehow, Al, I don't seem able to love beyond a certain stage. I'd give my last cent to any of the bunch and do anything on earth for them because I love 'em separately and severally, but I couldn't marry any of them. . . .

Henry had moved back into town and found a job working at a local pharmacy. Peggy sent him a letter while she was recuperating. It is undated and is contained in an unaddressed envelope, which leads one to speculate that perhaps it was hand-delivered by a friend.

Listen, old dear, I fibbed to you. No, I plain lied, and I can't keep a lie on my conscience. No, it's nothing very big but I'm rather proud of our record for veracity. It was about that joke you told Red W.—you remember? Well, he did tell me. So I'm a hot liar. Please forgive me.

I've been wanting to write you but I been feeling punker than punk since coming home— just don't seem to have any pep.

Besides, it's darned lonesome after the hospital. Besides, I got a letter from Court giving me hell. It makes me ill. I'm going to write and give her the same.

I've felt you thinking of me lots since I've been home, particu-

larly at night, and I do miss you! Don't be blue, my dear, take every day as it comes and try to make the most of it. That's what I'm trying to do. I must stop as I'm sick from mixing drags and milk—

> Your
>
> Peg

[SEPTEMBER 15, 1921]

Thursday p.m. 12:30

Henry dear—I called and called you tonight and then made Dr. Morris take me up to North Avenue to buy a toothbrush in hopes of seeing you. But you weren't there. I'm terribly sorry for I wanted to see you before I left. It is after midnight now and I still have my stuff to pack. I have to get up at 5, so I'm going to make this short, honey. If you see Ed Cooper I wish you [to] ask him to stop telling folks that Red and I are figuring an early marriage. It isn't so and I don't appreciate his efforts on my behalf worth a darn.

Henry, they didn't know what size your Kodak took and I couldn't get film. I'm going to send you enough for three rolls—when I find out my address—and could you send 'em? Also a few stray .320 not many.

Henry, I thank you for offering your .22 but I know how you prize it and I'd have a fit if anything happened to it.

Wish me luck, my dear. I'm

going to try very hard to stage a last "come back."

Love to Dave and your Mother—To you, too.

Peg.

Some of Margaret "Peggy" Mitchell's letters to Henry Love Angel create more mysteries than they solve. What was Mitchell's "come back"? Where was she going that Henry offered her the use of his rifle?

In the spring of 1922, Peggy is in Birmingham, Alabama. She appears to take a voluntary job at the *Birmingham News,* where her friend Augusta Dearborn worked in the society office. This undated four-page letter, written on *Birmingham News* letterhead, must have been painful for Henry to receive: in it she tells him that she cannot accept his proposal of marriage.

Henry Dear—

My eyes have been giving me hell since arriving here. They really have me worried. I have purchased a green eye shade [visor] that I wear constantly, but that doesn't seem to do much good. Wish you'd ask Doc Reed if there's anything on God's green earth to do or take. It doesn't matter whether I use my eyes or not, I have the most blinding headaches. I loaded up on [aspirin] 'til I'm really afraid to take more—only an enormous amount has any effect anyway. I'd appreciate it, dear, if you'd tell the doc and write me what he says. I thought the change might help me to sleep and every thing, but I'm awake much as ever.

But enough weeps. I'm having a good time. Augusta works on this paper and I'm in charge of the society office now, as she is out. Thank goodness, she isn't trying to give me a wild rush as I gave her in Atlanta; it's mostly a family affair (she has three brothers). We go out if we want to but mostly stay fer bums—which suits me admirably as I'm so stupid on account of my head.

Dear, do what you think best about making money, in the way you spoke. You know what I mean—don't you? In a way, I feel badly about your being broke last month—for I was a bit responsible for it—wasn't I? Between me 'n' the man who borrowed the $25 bucks? Well, dear, after all, money isn't every thing, tho' God knows, it's a lot—peace of mind and self respect mean a bit more—and dear if you can have the peace of mind and the respect as well as the crooked money (I'm not meaning "crooked" in a mean way, dear; I merely use that term for lack of a better one), well, then go ahead. It's your happiness, I want, dear and if money and the old life of likker, gambling and women will give you a measure of happiness, then I'm for you. I want to see you happy, and Henry, for God's sake, if I ever say I care about you—or feel just the same toward you except that I can't marry you, please take my word for it—and not the word of any Doc L or Edwin L or any other prying son-of-a-gun whose sole object is curiosity. I do love you, old timer, and feel you are my boy as long as you want to be my boy.

I must stop now, my eyes hurt—Henry, could you call Susie and see if she has discontinued my cream? If not, tell her to do so—and also to forward any mail to me. Thanks.

Love,

Peggy.

If Peggy would not marry Henry, she wasn't above borrowing money from him. Postmarked on February 23, 1922, her next letter shows once again the loving suitor has complied with her requests, perhaps ignoring her previous comments about not marrying him.

Dear—

I'd have written you sooner but have been down with ptomaine poisoning plus the C [cramps]. The former was a light case, due to eating aspic that had set 24 hours in a tin pan. The latter was terrible, dear—so much so that it frightened me as I wondered if after all, I wasn't getting better. I haven't been so bad off in years and I am still weak.

Thank you so much for Doc Reed's stuff. It was good of you to special it. When you see the Doc—speak to him thusly, boric acid does no good as the trouble doesn't involve the eyes them selves.

The capsules were good and eased the pain.

Calomel and salts are two things that tear me up. Besides as I am away from home so much, it would be very inconvenient.

Any way, the blinding headaches stopped as suddenly as they began, leaving only the dull, stupid sensation.

Dear, when I first received the proceeds from the jewels, I fully intend[ed] to send it back to you and tell you to go get the "jewels" as I know how you hate to have it away from you—But, dear, being a visitor is more expensive than I thought and I needed it just then—so my good intentions were for naught. Honey, I do appreciate your sending it to me (when God knows you needed it!) more than I would a hundred times that—from anybody else—no soft soap, dear. You are very sweet to me and it makes me very happy that there is some body in the world like you that I can always depend on—for the little things of life and the Big things too.

Give love to your mother. Believe I'll be home next week if my head is no better. Write to me.

Love, Peggy

The intrepid Margaret "Peggy" Mitchell strikes
a bold pose in front of her Atlanta home.

*Henry Angel and Peggy Mitchell appear in what may be
their last photograph taken together.*

Less than a week later, Peggy Mitchell announced her return home in another letter.

[ENVELOPE POSTMARKED MARCH 1, 1922, BUT THE LETTER IS UNDATED]

Dear—

I think I will be home Thursday on the afternoon train. B'ham has been lovely but I've missed the old town more than I thought I could. I have to go down and buy me some stockings so I'll have to close this. It's only a note to tell you I'm coming home—and that I've missed you.

Love,

Peggy

Peggy did return to Atlanta in the spring of 1922. But later that June she was back in Alabama, staying at a "plantation" owned by her suitor Winston "Red" Withers. Losing his hold on the affections of his life's first true love must have been painful for Henry. The following letter from Mitchell discloses that she was not unaware of this suffering. The letter is postmarked Greensboro, Alabama, June 26, 1922, 6:30 P.M., and the back of the envelope reads: MMM, c/o W. R. Withers, Greensboro, Ala.

[THE TOP LEFT CORNER READS]

p.s. If you have that letter of Court's that I gave you ages ago, please destroy it.

[THE TOP RIGHT CORNER READS]

Sat June 24, '22

Greensboro, Ala.

My dear—

I wondered, before I left if you were sore at me and why. I wondered why you didn't call me up to tell me the result of Doc Reed's examination of you. I thought you'd realize how anxious I was to know how you came out. As you didn't let me know anything, I phoned you from Nunnelly's sometime later. I wanted to see you, that day. But you talked rather strangely—a bit embarrassed as 'twere, and didn't seem a bit desirous of seeing me—So I said nothing, my dear. It hurt me to think that you believed I didn't care or wasn't interested in your health, particularly that. Several times before leaving town, I called you as I wanted to have lunch with you—but, you never were in—and finally, I figured you'd call me if you wanted to see me. The day I left town, I saw you with some girl—(I did not see her face but she looked quite attractive—). I yelled at you but you didn't see me, I guess.

Are you sore at me? Or has Grace or some other girl so filled your mind that you've forgotten me? Or do you think that my love for Red has changed me in any degree toward you? I'd really like to know, my dear, for I hate to think of there being a barrier between us.

I have been on Red's plantation so long that I've gotten fat. It's a lazy life. And it is hot as blue blazes. I don't do much but eat, sleep and swim. Wish to God I could ride as Red has some beautiful horses but Doc Reed's ultimatum on the subject of horses was absolute. This has certainly done me good as it's the longest stretch in two years that I've

been minus a tummy ache. From here I'm
going over to St. Simons where Augusta's
sister has a cottage. If this keeps up, I
thought I'd be well by this fall—for which,
my dear, I'll be thankful. Red sends you
his very best—we have talked of you lots
these last four nights, wonder if you
thought of us?

What about a letter, dear?

Love

Peggy

Henry had never envisioned marrying
anyone but Peggy, but he began to resign himself, and earlier in the
spring he had met someone else, a young central telephone operator at
the Hemlock exchange named Grace Rayfield. Eventually she would
steal his heart.

Peggy did go to St. Simons Island with Augusta Dearborn in July,
but Red Upshaw was there, too. We do not know when Henry became
aware of John Marsh, but about six months earlier Marsh wrote his

sister about meeting Peggy. Sometime in
the summer of 1922, Atlanta gossip about
Peggy's love life was made louder by a
revealing newspaper photograph of Peggy
Mitchell, John Marsh, and Red Upshaw,
and by the end of July, her upcoming marriage was announced.

Perhaps Henry finally accepted his
rejection when Peggy married Red

Upshaw on September 2, 1922. However, he did save another letter dated September 20, 1922. Peggy and Red had just returned to Atlanta from their honeymoon at the Grove Park Inn in Asheville, North Carolina.

Tuesday

Henry Dear—

I got home yesterday morning and tried to call you up—but it was a miserable failure as I have some thing wrong with my tonsils, pus pockets, Doc Reed calls them, that have affected my vocal cords so that I just can whisper. I wanted to say hello to your mother too but central couldn't even hear me! Talk about iodine tasting like a rusty nail— well, I hate to tell you what this silver nitrate with which he is painting my tonsils, tastes like.

Henry, what is Skeet's address? I want to thank him for the Dirty Three emblem which now adorns the front hall table. It's or rather they are as pretty as can be and I'm thanking you over again for them, tho I've thanked you once before.

Henry, I'm quite shameless in asking you to take me out to lunch sometime this week! I not only want to see you, but I have something of yours to give you.

Love

Peggy

We will never know if they went to lunch that week. But we do know that only a short time later Peggy discovered that she had made a mistake marrying Red Upshaw. She kicked him out of the house by the next summer and received her final divorce decree in 1924. During the interim, she started work as a reporter and found more comfort in the arms of John Marsh, whom she later married.

Within three months of Peggy's wedding, Henry applied for a marriage license, and he and Grace were married on December 9, 1922. They took up residence in the house next door to his parents, who lived one street away from Peggy and her family. Henry Angel Jr. was born in December 1924, and his brother William was born several years later. Henry Jr. recalls Margaret Mitchell stopping by throughout his childhood, remembering in particular a time when she arrived with friends, autographed a copy of *Gone With the Wind*, and gave it to them.

Late in 1944, Henry became ill and required repeated trips to the hospital for a respiratory illness. Henry Jr. remembers that his father smoked and drank a lot. In March 1945, Henry Love Angel died; he was only forty-four. Although the primary cause of death on Henry's death certificate has been obliterated by time, the secondary causes were lung cancer and congestive heart failure. Henry died taking his secret to the grave, without so much as a mention of Margaret Mitchell to his adult sons. Never once did he breathe a word about his past relationship with Margaret Mitchell. Never once did he seek gain from her celebrity. Perhaps it was for the sake of love and honor that Henry Love Angel kept silent. The world was different then in some respects: a handshake could seal a contract, a person's word was his bond, and a woman's honor was prized above all else.

Margaret Mitchell died four years later, less than three months from her forty-ninth birthday. Her untimely death was caused by injuries she sustained when struck by a car as she crossed Peachtree Street.

Henry Jr. remembers the last time he saw Margaret Mitchell. It was at his grandparents' home, about a year after his father's death. "She just sat there and looked at me. I remember thinking, 'Why is she staring at me? Is my hair not combed or something?' But then she told me, 'You look just like your daddy.' " It would be years before he learned his father's secret and understood.

Two questions will always exist. Why didn't Peggy marry Henry Love Angel? Why did Henry save these mementos?

There is one final letter that Henry saved among his keepsakes. Undated, it will forever remain a mystery.

Henry—come back tonight.
Peggy.

NOTES

∞

PREFACE

page

7. In 1916, Margaret: Freer, p. 56.

7. He is not: ibid., p. 56.

7. In Margaret Mitchell's own will there is no request that her writings be destroyed, but in her husband John Marsh's will he stated that she requested their destruction and mentions the items destroyed, including the original *Gone With the Wind* material. The destruction of Margaret Mitchell's writings and personal papers was first carried out by her husband and, after his death, by her brother Stephens Mitchell.

8. In August 1994, I was told by the Road to Tara Museum's president Patsy Wiggins that Henry Angel Jr. called and approached the museum about his late father's letters, photos, etc. In September, Angel visited the museum with a few of the items he was offering for sale. The museum then asked me to meet with Angel and look at what he had. During this interview, the items were displayed on a kitchen table. The negatives and photographs were in a shoe box with Angel's other personal photos and required tedious sorting, since he had not determined or isolated those of Mitchell or her other friends. Many of these prints had been recently made from these negatives and there was no accounting for the number of copies made or their whereabouts. There were fifteen pieces of correspondence, including wedding invitations to the Courtenay Ross and Helen Turman weddings. The contents of the story in two composition books were unknown at that time. Angel also stated that there was a ring kept with these items, but its whereabouts were unknown. Angel was asked many questions about his family and the history of these items. He also revealed that at one time he had thought of selling Mitchell's *Lost Laysen* to a magazine like *Redbook* but was concerned about Stephens Mitchell.

8. "What do I": Angel Jr.

9. "what was written": Marsh, p. 42.

10-11. Additional similarities exist between *Lost Laysen* and *Gone With the Wind*, but only a few are specifically noted in the text; another parallel exists between the *GWTW* passage about the assault on Tony Fontaine's sister-in-law and avenging her honor and *Laysen's* passage about Courtenay's assault, with Steele and Duncan seeking revenge. There are also other similarities between Mitchell's own life and that of her fiction besides those mentioned in this paragraph.

INTRODUCTION

page

14. stories as soon as . . . words: Harwell, *Atlanta Historical Journal*, p. 27.

14. "She always scowled . . .": Shavin and Shartar, p. 7.

14. *The Traitor:* Peacock, p. 15.

14. Steve: Farr, p. 159.

15. "Steve Hoyle": corresponding photographs in Mitchell Marsh Collection, University of Georgia.

15. "Siamese twins . . . 'D.T.' for short": Peacock, p. 13.

16-17. School photographs: *Facts and Fancies,* courtesy of the Atlanta History Center.

16. accepting dates: Courtenay Ross McFadyen, 1980 audio interview.

16. Red Upshaw: Pyron, pp. 131–32.

17-18. "Scrambling briskly out . . . rocky island": *Facts and Fancies*, 1917–18.

18. Henry Jr., recalls: He also stated that Henry Love Angel worked in a garage downtown; the carburetor design was possibly in the 1930s, but Ford already held the patent.

18. "out with Courtenay": Peacock, p. 90.

22. promoted to sergeant: Angel Jr., and witnessed by original document.

22. According to army historians, service ended at the conclusion of the war unless there was a specific need for reenlistment. Henry was honorably discharged for "industrial reasons" in July 1919.

22. Descriptions of Shadowbrook Farm were from private photographs and the reminiscences of George B. Wilkins as written by his son Barratt Wilkins. George W. Wilkins was the father of Shadowbrook guests Phyllis, George B., and Bernard Wilkins and friend of Victor L. Smith. Both Wilkins and Smith were officers of the Atlanta Music Festival Association, which brought the Metropolitan Opera to Atlanta. Wilkins, through his company Cable Piano, was also a major sponsor of Washington Seminary's theatrical productions, which featured players Margaret Mitchell and Courtenay Ross.

22. According to Gwinnett County Tax Digests, 1890–1923, during this 1919–20 period Victor L. Smith (1867–1947) owned a gentleman's farm of about 800 acres. According to published accounts, Smith and his first wife, Caroline Johnston Smith (who had worked at the Red Cross), had recently moved their residence from Atlanta to Shadowbrook. However, approximately three years after the untimely death of Mrs. Smith in 1919, Shadowbrook Farm ceased to exist as it had been known and seen in the photographs.

24. The photograph caption refers to a ring that Mitchell is wearing. According to Angel Jr., a ring was kept with these letters, composition books, and photos when he received them. Although mentioned during interviews, the ring was later separated from the materials and misplaced before the materials were acquired by the museum. The Angel family was unable to locate the ring by the time of this writing. Worth noting is that during the Depression, other family jewelry was sold, but not this ring.

32. "Angel proposing . . . guess the answer?": Summers. Jessie Summers is the daughter of Jessie Brown, who together with her sisters Frances and Ruth Brown (former Washington Seminary classmate) were friends of Margaret Mitchell.

36. Identification of the gang at House Party #3 was made possible with help from Dorothy Reeves, daughter of Mitchell friend Phyllis Wilkins, and other private photographs.

36. "a pair of stolen boys' trousers": Summers.

38-39. In Mitchell's letter, the dramatic passage about the flag-draped coffin on the platform has always struck Henry Jr. as a haunting reminder of a similar scene in *GWTW*.

40. On October 8, a theater party was given: Peacock, p. 107; note that Peacock records the other host's name as Hitchock, however the name was a misspelling of Hiscox.

43. Photograph of Margaret Mitchell wearing her Apache dance costume for the Mi-Careme Ball, from the Mitchell Marsh Collection. Photograph courtesy of Hargrett Rare Book and Manuscript Library, University of Georgia Libraries, Stephens Mitchell Trust.

47-48. "As to who was in my room . . . but I couldn't marry any of them": Peacock, excerpted letter, Mitchell to Edee, pp. 116–19.

57. "[Marsh] wrote his sister": Walker, pp. 10–11.

58. Although many of Margaret Mitchell's letters mention her various health problems, Mitchell seemed to be accident-prone. Courtenay denied the possibility of Mitchell being a hypochondriac, stating "that her friend was always 'embarrassed to be sick' ": Peacock, p. 15.

59. kicked him out of the house: Pyron, p. 141.

59. autographed a copy of *Gone With the Wind*; smoked and drank a lot: Angel Jr.

59. Henry Love Angel's marriage license and death certificate: Fulton County Probate Court and Fulton County Health Department.

Photograph of the composition book cover in which Margaret
Mitchell wrote the first half of <u>Lost Laysen</u>. Mitchell concluded
the work in a second composition book labeled "Book II."

Lost Laysen

c h a p t e r

o n e

ill Duncan settled back in his chair and lit his pipe. I said nothing but waited for him to speak for I knew that the usually taciturn Irishman was going to tell me something worth hearing.

"Well, boy, you say that all romance and adventure died with Cap'n Kidd? Well, it didn't." He paused and gazed out of the window into the black tropical night. All the night sounds and smells, so new and strange to my New York self,

drifted into me and my imagination began to people the darkness outside with all manner of beasts
and men.

"Well, it didn't," repeated Duncan abruptly.
"Do you remember Lost Laysen?"

I nodded, my interest rising. There were only
a few who remembered several notices in the papers
of the disappearance, fifteen years ago, of Laysen,
a volcanic island of the Tongas group. It had been
a large island peopled mostly by Japanese, Chinese
and a few whites.

"Well," continued Duncan slowly, "fifteen
years ago, I was first mate on the 'Caliban,' a little
old tub that carried passengers and did trading
among the Tongas. It was a hell of a work, Charley
boy, trading among those islands and never knowing when I was going to get a Jap knife between my
shoulders. It was fight all the time, but I liked it,
then. I guess I was forgetting that I was a white
man and turning yellow when—<u>she</u> came. She took
passage at Yindano for Laysen and the minute I
laid eyes on her, I knew I could never forget her.
It wasn't any joke, boy," he said as I grinned at the

thought of this rough fellow cherishing any sen-
timental thought, "I hadn't seen a woman from
God's country—a good woman—in so long, that
maybe I'd forgotten there were such things."

He puffed thoughtfully for a while and a soft
light over spread his weather beaten face. "Charley
boy, I sure did love that little woman, I couldn't
help it, tho I knew I never had a chance—she
wasn't my kind. I wonder why it's always the little
women that appeal to us big fellows? She wasn't
much over five feet and she couldn't have weighed
115! Why I could have carried her in one hand and
never known it! But I wouldn't have laid hands on
her for all the world. Her eyes would have kept
anybody from doing that. They were grey-blue eyes
and she looked at you as straight and steady as a
man without any coquetry or anything like that.
She had a strong straight nose and a Cupid's bow
mouth. You don't see mouths like that often,
Charley boy, the kind that were made for kissing.

"When I first saw her come up the gangplank
at Yindano, I could only stare at her. I was a tough
looking customer in those days. Tougher than I am

now," he laughed harshly and the sound grated
on my nerves, "I'd just come out of a fight and my
head and hand were tied up in some dirty ban-
dages so I looked worse than usual. I just stood
and looked at her, like the fool I was 'till she got
on deck and put down her bag. When she turned
to face me, I had a minute of politeness left and I
snatched off my cap—a thing which I hadn't done
to a woman in 5 years. Her quick grey eyes ran over
me and then she grinned. Yes, Charley boy, grinned!
It wasn't one of those simpering smiles, but a plain
honest grin that I couldn't help returning."

"Say, you must have been in a fight!" she said
and then laughed. The captain came up just then,
laughing, for he had heard what she said.

" 'Duncan's always fighting, Miss Ross, he isn't
happy unless he's in a scrap!' "

"I could feel myself grow red as her twinkling
eyes sought the dirty rag around my head and I
could have murdered the captain then and there
for his words. Even tho they were true, I hated to
have her know it. But I couldn't have said anything
if my life had depended on it. I just kept wishing

that I had shaved off a week's beard and washed
my face that morning. But the captain took her off
to show her her little cubbyhole of a cabin and
left me leaning against the rail. I watched her 'till
she disappeared and just then I noticed how trim
and neat she looked in her dark blue suit, with her
boy's Buster Brown collar. But she was so <u>little</u>,
Charley boy, <u>so</u> <u>little</u>." Duncan stopped to light
his pipe which had gone out. Five feet did not
seem so small to me—I was 5 ft 6, but Duncan was
at least 6 ft 3, of hard bunchy muscle. "Well, I dived
for my cabin and was making preparations for a
hasty shave when the captain walked in. You should
have heard him laugh when he saw my face covered
with lather. That laugh riled me, Charley boy, and
I began to curse. Don't look so astonished, the Cap
and I were great pals and there wasn't any disci-
pline between us."

"'Oh! see pretty Bill Duncan cleaning up for
the missionary!'" he jeered.

I stopped short. "She's no missionary!"

"Oh, yes she is," grinned the Cap.

"Hell!" I said and put down my razor. You see,

I didn't have a very good opinion of missionaries then and for pretty good reasons.

"How do you come to know so much about her?" I snapped.

All the grin left the Cap's face and his mouth straightened out like an iron nail.

"Never you mind," he said, "but I do."

Charley boy, I'd been with Jim Harrison 5 years and I'd never asked him anything about himself. Over here in the East, it's not etiquette to ask a man his past history, but I know that Miss Ross and her class of people had played a part in the Cap's past. But I asked no questions. In a minute, he spoke again.

"Bill, she's of the best America has and she's over here because she's tired of the life over there. Her family were fools to let her come here. She wants excitement and believe me, she'll get it." He stopped and then laughed—"Missionary? My Lord, Bill, she's about as psalm singing as you are!"

"Where is she going?"

"To Laysen," he said grimly.

"Lord Jim, we can't let her go <u>there</u>. It's hell on

earth and those Japs are devils—" I began angrily.

"How are you going to stop her?" growled the
Cap, "She's her own boss. All we can do is keep an
eye on her—and you'll be glad to do that—won't
you—Billy Duncan?" And, giving me a punch in
the ribs, he fled.

Well, I shaved and washed and got a clean rag
around my head and went up on deck. Charley
boy, you've never been away from women—good
women—for five years so you don't know how I
felt. I just wanted to see her, to hear her, to be near
her. I didn't realize that I loved her then, I only
knew that I wanted to look down into her steady
grey eyes and to see her red lips move. She was on
deck when I got there, watching the Chinese load
our little tub, and the captain was beside her,
explaining things. There didn't seem to be any
other passengers at Yindano so we were the only
white people on the boat, with a crew of 16—Japs,
Chinks, Kanakas and half breeds. When I came up
to them, the Cap introduced us and even then I
couldn't say anything. She gave me a straight from
the waist hand shake and I must have nearly broke

her little hand with my big paw. When the loading was finished, Captain Harrison sent me to the wheel to head the "Caliban" out of the harbor. I had gotten her well out of Yindano and headed for sea when Miss Ross rushed in like a whirlwind.

"Say, have you got a pair of glasses?" she demanded and then seeing my glasses hanging in their case on the wall she grabbed them up and looked landward for a moment. She evidently saw something very funny for she began to explode with laughter and double up as with a cramp. The captain came in then and giving the wheel to him, I caught the glasses from her hands and looked back at Yindano. There on the wharf we had just left was a crowd of natives and in front of them, clad in white trousers, blue coat and Panama hat, a man was running up and down making wild signals, evidently to us! I was puzzled and handed the glasses to the Cap. Miss Ross seemed almost on the verge of hysterics and tears trembled in her eyes. "It's Douglas Steele!" she gasped, slapping her knee in the manner of a man. "He didn't want me—to come out here—and he would follow me!

I gave him the slip at 'Frisco and there he is! I'm so glad he got left! Doesn't he look funny?" and she went off into another gale of laughter that left her weak.

"Maybe we'd better go back for him!" said the Cap gravely, giving me a wink. She sat bolt upright.

"No you don't!" she cried, "It serves him right. Doug is a good fellow. But he's altogether too officious!" And taking the glasses from the Cap, she staggered weakly to the rail and looked shoreward again.

"Can you beat it?" murmured the Cap.

"No," I said truthfully. "Who is Douglas Steele, Jim?"

"You ought to read more papers Bill," grunted the Captain, "He's son of D. G. Steele, the arms manufacturer but he's one of the big athletes of America—sprints, swings hammers, pole vaults, does high jumps—but I can't see why he's following Courtenay Ross all over creation."

"Courtenay," I repeated and didn't say anything else for I was thinking what a pretty name hers was and how well it suited her.

I didn't see her much that afternoon for I was at the wheel but when we got to Buna—(Buna was one of the islands we did most of our trading with) she said she was going ashore with the Cap. Somehow, the boat seemed dull and empty without her, Charley boy, and I couldn't help wishing I was ashore with her. We had only two hours to stay at Buna and as we were a day behind our schedule, I got off my coat and shirt and began to help those lazy natives unloading as they were taking all day about it. I had intended to get on my clothes, long before Miss Ross and the captain came back but time flew by. I was handling boxes and cursing those natives when I chanced to look up. There on the rail of the ship not much above my head was perched Miss Ross, her chin in hand, eagerly watching. I stopped short—inwardly cursing myself, for when once in my life, I had wanted to make a good impression on a woman, that woman found me half naked and swearing like a pirate. I could only look up at her helplessly. I didn't mind so much for myself but I didn't want to embarrass her. She did not laugh or blush but there was a world of seriousness in her eyes.

"Mr. Duncan," she said softly, "If I were a man, I'd give anything to have shoulders and muscles like yours," she slipped off the rail and then flung back over her shoulder with a laugh—"And such a vocabulary, too!"

I was just hurriedly getting into my clothes when up sailed a miserable cockleshell of a craft that I wouldn't have trusted my life in for a second. There were two natives in it and one white man, the same man who I had seen on the wharf at Yindano. As the boat drew closer I saw that he was a good looking young fellow of about 23, tall, broad of shoulder and lean of hips. He eyed the "Caliban" anxiously as he came along side and a sudden pain shot thru me. It wasn't jealousy, Charley, it was just plain selfishness. I knew, I could never have her and so I didn't want anyone to. Moreover, I knew that if a man thinks enough of a woman to follow her from the States to this God forsaken place he would not be the man to be easily discouraged in his suit. When the cockleshell drew up at the wharf, the white man sprang out, lifted his valise from the bottom of the boat and then paid the two natives. He drew a deep sigh of relief as he looked at the "Caliban" and seeing me buttoning up my coat, he questioned anxiously, "Is Miss Courtenay Ross on that boat?"

I nodded for I was in no mood for wasting words. I was just wishing that I could look as clean, inside and out as he did. He didn't wait for further words but ran up the gangplank. A minute later I heard a startled exclamation, a peal of laughter and words of greeting. I had the ropes cast off and headed the "Caliban" for open sea but the pain in my heart was so strong that it was only a miracle that I did not run the ship on the reefs.

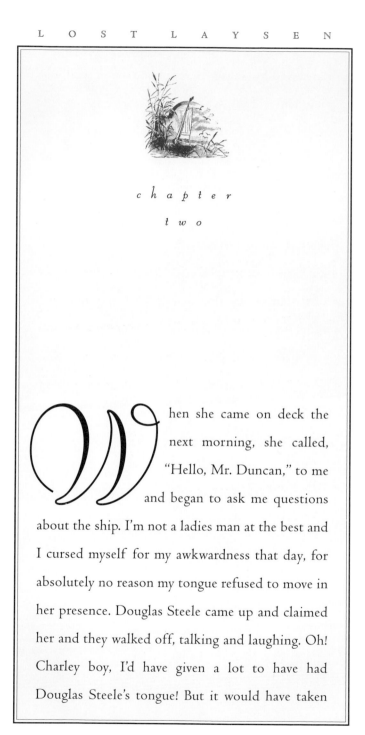

c h a p t e r

t w o

hen she came on deck the next morning, she called, "Hello, Mr. Duncan," to me and began to ask me questions about the ship. I'm not a ladies man at the best and I cursed myself for my awkwardness that day, for absolutely no reason my tongue refused to move in her presence. Douglas Steele came up and claimed her and they walked off, talking and laughing. Oh! Charley boy, I'd have given a lot to have had Douglas Steele's tongue! But it would have taken a greater tongue than his to have told her of the thoughts in my brain.

At the next little island we touched, we got several passengers, all natives. We were about to leave when a slim, dark man came on board. His eyes narrowed when he saw me for if ever anyone hated me, that man was the one. He was a half breed—Jap and Spanish—possessing the devils own dark beauty. He had soft black eyes that slanted slightly and a soft, red woman's mouth that always sneered. His hair was soft and black and silky and his yellow brown skin was soft. Oh! he <u>looked</u> soft and gentle all right but if ever there was a fiend out of Hell, it was Juan Mardo. He had great influence among the islands, and especially at Laysen where he lived, for he was the richest man, white or native, for miles around. And he hated the captain and me because we'd stopped quite a few of his murder and kidnapping parties. He came on deck without a word and just then Miss Ross and Douglas Steele passed. Miss Ross looked back over her shoulder at him—merely a bit of feminine curiosity I suppose—for he <u>was</u>

good to look at. But the look he gave her made my blood boil. He shrugged his shoulders and made a remark in Japanese to the man next to him—a remark so vile that only a dog of a Jap could have thought it.

I understood Japanese and Juan Mardo knew it. The look he gave her had been a strain on my self control but his remark about that little lady drove me into a blind fury. I caught the dog around the waist and flung him across the deck. As I did, three of the latest passengers closed in on me and I had my hands full. I was fighting desperately and my blows taking some effect when I heard her voice from somewhere.

"Go it Billy Duncan! Slam him in the jaw," and then, "Don't you help him, Douglas, he can clean them up by himself!"

I grinned even in my rage. What a little firebrand she was! Most women would have screamed or fainted. I laid one native flat on the deck and was preparing to do the same for the other two, when one clutched me around the knees and the other got an arm about the front of my neck in a half-nelson. Things were beginning to go black and little bright spots leaped before my eyes but I heard her yelling like a demon—

"Break that nelson, Billy Duncan, break it— break it! Break it! You nearly did it—go to it!" and then swift alarm leaping into her voice—"Oh! Doug! He's got a knife! Stop him!"

Thru burning eyes, I saw Juan Mardo pick himself up and come at me with his knife. I thought that I was gone that time for I was as helpless as a kid and my chest looked tempting to that half-breed. All went dark for a moment and then I heard Captain Jim Harrison's roar of rage, Douglas Steele's curse and felt the sharp bite of steel in my shoulder, almost simultaneously the two Kanakas let go me and blind to everything else, I went for Juan Mardo, all forgetful of his knife. I got him by the throat at last, but I felt his knife in my arm three times before I did. I guess I would have choked the life out of him there on the deck, for I was aching to kill him bare handed, not for the little knife pricks he had given me but for what he had said about her. It was for her I was fighting and there had been a fierce joy in every blow I had given in that fight.

I could feel Juan Mardo growing limp in my hands when a little hand with steel fingers clamped on my shoulder and her voice came authoritatively, "Get up, Billy Duncan."

I got up instantly, involuntarily. If she'd said "go to hell!" that way, I'd have gone there straight. But as I stood before her, all torn and dirty and blood stained, I never felt so like a kid in my life. I sure did regret my bigness and roughness then for I knew she'd think me only a tough—which I was, undoubtedly. The Cap and Steele had finished their men and they came up, Steele all excited and Jim mad as hell.

"Billy Duncan, is it impossible for you to keep out of a fight for five minutes? Why did you start this one and with <u>him</u>?" he growled.

I snapped back at him in Jap and told what Mardo had said. He smiled quietly for he didn't want her to suspect anything but I saw murder in his eye. My right arm and shoulder began to throb then and I caught at the corner of the rail to hold upright for the deck swirled around in a most sickening way.

"Take him to my cabin," I heard her say as from afar off. I made some weak protest but the next thing I knew, I was sitting at her feet with my arm across her knees and she was cutting my shirt off. Steele and the Cap were gone. Her fingers were cool and quick and skillfully and in a very short while my arm was in a sling and my shoulder well bandaged. I sat at her feet, leaning against her knees, too tired to move and for the second time in two days before her without my shirt. I felt her cool hands slide over my shoulder with its hard packs of muscle and down my arm. I looked up into her eyes then and I caught a fleeting glance of pure terror in them. I couldn't make anything of it then but I realize now that it was my pure brute strength that she feared, for she did not know that I would have died a hundred deaths rather than harmed her.

"God made you well, Mr. Duncan," she said softly and as I said nothing she questioned swiftly, "Why did you fight that Spaniard, Mr. Duncan?"

I shook my head. I was feeling better but not much like talking as yet.

"Tell me!" she said imperatively but I shook my head again. "Was it about me?" she questioned. "What did he say?" softly pleading.

"I can not tell you," I replied tho I feared I would anger her. She did not speak for a minute and I began to fear that I had indeed angered her by my refusal. Then she dropped her hand to my head and began to gently rumple my hair just as mother used to do.

"Thank you, Billy Duncan," she said with a funny quiver in her voice, and looking up, I saw tears in her eyes. Ah! Charley boy, I was in Paradise then, with my head against her knee, her hand in my hair and tears in her eyes, for me! But I knew that the things I dreamed could never come true and with a sigh I started to rise. But with her hand on my shoulder, she pushed me back.

"Sit still, boy," she said, softly. Boy! Maybe that sounds funny to you, Charley with me 29 and she only 19 but it suddenly came to me that she saw the boy in all men and liked the boy in them

best. To her, all men were only boys. "Billy
Duncan, tell me about yourself," she said next as
she ran her cool hand over my hot forehead. It had
been hard to talk to her before but with her hand
on my forehead, my words came easily. I told her
how I had left Ireland at 16—left family, school
and friends. I had to leave because I was in a little
revolt and there was a price on my head. I told her
how I had wandered about the world, taking hard
knocks, getting little but hell out of life and always
fighting whenever there was a fight to be fought.
Her eyes glistened when I spoke of fights and
danger and I knew that a man's heart beat in that
woman's breast. When I finished, she sighed softly.

"You are a soldier of fortune; all right, Billy
Duncan," she said, and she felt my shoulder again,
"God made you well," she repeated.

"He gave me the brawn but not the brain," I
replied, bitterly and sank my head to her knee
again. All grew hazy after that and I fell asleep,
with her hand still on my head.

When I awoke the moonlight was shining into
the cabin and I was alone. I still sat on the floor

leaning against the chair but where her knee had been she had placed a pillow and she had wrapped a blanket about me. Rising, I reverently put the pillow and blanket back on the bed. How still, how moonlit that room was! It was so beautiful that it was holy and it was no place for me—Billy Duncan—Soldier of Fortune—Rolling Stone.

I was feeling better then. I was used to hard knocks and that sleep had done me a world of good. Still I was rather weak, as I went on deck and I had to hold to the rail as I made my way toward my cabin. It was a still night, not a bit of breeze to fill out sails and the "Caliban" stood still. I leaned against the mast in the white moonlight, listening to the crew wailing something down in their quarters and I thought of God's country— and her. It was then that I heard two voices— Douglas Steele's and hers—and looking around the mast I saw them on the other side of the ship, leaning against the rail talking. She was a beautiful sight to the poor woman-starved man that I was so I stood and looked at her watching the moonlight cast shadows about her face. She was dreamily looking at the silver trail the moon made across the water and scarcely listening to Douglas Steele.

"But, look here, Court," he was saying. "You can't stay out here! You are no missionary and you know it!"

"I <u>can</u> stay out here," she replied promptly, "I <u>am</u> a missionary and I'm going to wash dirty little Japs and teach 'em not to stick knives in people."

He threw up his hands in despair, "Court, you must come home! Court, you <u>know</u> I love you for the tenth time—won't you marry me?" He was smiling when he said the last but he was dead serious. Somehow the pain in my heart then, was sharper than the bite had been of Juan Mardo's knife. But not that I would have liked Douglas Steele to have had her, for if ever man loved woman he did her. But, oh! Charley boy, I wanted her so!

"No, Doug," she said quietly, "I've work to do here and I can not marry you."

I felt for Steele when he heard that but he threw back his shoulder and said just as quietly, "Then, I'll wait till your work is finished, little lady."

Little Lady! that was what I always thought of her as. She did not speak, then her eyes sparkled.

"Wasn't that one glorious scrap this afternoon?"

I could have laughed. How quickly her moods changed! She could be imperious—tender as a mother—like a giggling school girl—then possessing all the wisdom of centuries of women and full of enthusiasm and life as a little boy.

"It sure was," returned Steele. "That man is a born fighter."

"He's a mighty good fellow," she said and grinned in recollection.

"He's sure gone on you, little lady," he said lighting a cigarette. I started angrily at first but then I forgave him. It was true—his lover's eyes were sharp and besides we were almost in the same boat. I waited breathlessly to hear her reply.

"Don't be an idiot, Doug," she said.

"But he is, you can tell that by his eyes for he never uses his mouth. His eyes remind me of that Colly you had last year. He's a queer fellow—"

"He's a mighty good fellow," she repeated softly,

"He reminds me of a bulldog with that jaw of his. He's a good fellow, Doug, and it's a pity he's not more than he is. But he never had a chance—good night, Doug, I'm going to bed." And she left him alone in the moonlight.

God! How selfish he was. He wanted all of her and I—I'd have died for a kiss—or lived a life of hell for a lock of her gold brown hair.

c h a p t e r

t h r e e

e made Laysen the next
morning and tho we had
only an hours stay there we
took the little lady and Douglas
Steele into the town. You see, Charley, Laysen was
a pretty big island but there was only one town on
it—and it was a miserable, fever struck, swampy
place. Japs lived all over the island, so did the
natives but the few white planters lived near the
town. The Cap and I took the two up to Senora
Castro, who took lodgers. The senora was a great

scoundrel tho a good natured one and her prices
were exorbitant. But Miss Ross and Steele paid
without a murmur. Evidently they were used to
more expensive things at home and fancied themselves getting off easily.

Captain Jim knew most of the white planters
at Laysen intimately and he wrote several letters of
introduction for them. I sat out under a bamboo
while he wrote for I was weak from yesterday's
fight. Soon she came out.

"Mr. Duncan, I think you might have given
us some letters of introduction, too!" she cried
jokingly.

"Letters, from me?" I said, trying to laugh. "If
the letter was from me I'm afraid they'd throw you
out, Miss R——."

"Can't you call me Courtenay?" She laughed
as she flung herself on the grass.

"Courtenay!" Call her by her first name?
Somehow I could not do it.

"No," I murmured awkwardly, "I can't. To me,
you are always the 'Little Lady.'" I stopped, feeling like a fool and almost fearing I had angered

her or she might laugh.

But she only looked straight at me with her steady grey eyes and said—"Thank you, Billy Duncan."

I was rather confused for I didn't know what she was thanking me for but I rose hastily. She got up, too. I looked down the hot street to where the naked brown children were rolling and at the yellow and brown men who smoked on doorsteps and in a rush it came over me that she was almost alone—she and Douglas Steele—the only white faces in a sea of brown and yellow. A warning against that half breed fiend, Juan Mardo, leaped to my lips but I kept back. There had been that in his eyes as he watched her leave the boat that morning that would have made a white man joyfully kill him slowly by inches. Charley boy, I knew Japs. I hadn't lived in the East five years without knowing that a Jap holds a woman's life and honor at less than nothing, and Juan Mardo had set his eye on my little lady. I wanted to tell her but then I thought that it could do no good and maybe harm as I said nothing. But she was quick and had read something in my eyes.

"What were you going to say?" she jerked out.

I started and then smiled. "Only this, little lady—if you ever want anything or need anything— especially help—you'll know where to get it."

She smiled—it wasn't a grin this time—but just a smile that made me feel that she could see my soul and I wished to God my soul had been cleaner.

"I'll know where to find it," she put out her hand, "and I thank you."

I took her hand—a small, sturdy hand with tapering fingers—and as never before did I want to kiss it. But I was a fool—I knew it then as well as I do now and dropping her hand abruptly I went down the street toward the "Caliban."

It was two weeks before I saw her again and then it was only to say "hello." She, Douglas Steele and a gay party of the white planters were sailing in a pretty, little, white sailboat, about an hour out from Laysen, Douglas Steele was at the wheel, all cool in his white suit and she stood near him in a white middy and skirt. The whole party (there were about seven or eight) hailed us merrily as we passed, all I heard [was] her voice, ring[ing] clearly above them all—

"Hello, Billy Duncan!"

The Cap leaned over the rail and called "How's the missionary?" and the whole party roared.

She looked grieved but wrinkling her nose, she yelled back, "I'm getting along fine, don't you worry!"

So they sailed by us, a gay party laughing and chattering—Captain Harrison's kind—Steele's kind but not Billy Duncan's kind.

I think the Captain had a hunch of what was in my mind for I caught the half pitying glance he gave me as I turned away. I didn't want pity from any man—not even my best friend—the only thing on earth I wanted was—her. I longed for her as a man perishing of thirst longs for water. My longing amounted to a great hunger for her—for I wanted her so much.

The next time I saw her was two weeks later when the Cap and some Chinks carried me sense-less into Laysen. Of course I didn't see her while

I was in dreamland but I did afterward. You see, I had been in a fight aboard the "Caliban" and I had gotten the worst of it. The Cap had given me up in disgust for he had already discovered that I could not keep out of a row—that I had no desire of keeping out of one. Anyway, I had my head laid open by a belaying pin and that finished my side of the fight. Captain Jim had thrown a bucket of water over me—just as he usually did but this time it had no effect on me. He began to get anxious when I did not come around in the usual time so he put into Laysen where he knew there was a white doctor. I never found out what happened next but when I woke up two hours later, the "Caliban" was out to sea and I lay in a little hut opposite Senora Castro's with a pale, slim little fellow working over me. My head was aching terribly, so I didn't take notice of anything much at first, except that the little doctor seemed mighty relieved to see my eyes open. But when the doctor turned away and spoke to someone beside him and that someone's clear voice cried thankfully—

"Then he's all right, Doc?" All the pain and

dizziness seemed to leave me, I tried to sit up then but the little doctor laughed and pushed me back.

"You can't kill his kind, Miss Ross," he said as he began to pack things into his black leather bag. "Inside of two hours, he'll be as good as ever and when Captain Harrison comes by tomorrow, he'll be ready to go."

Things grew rather hazy then but I dimly heard the door close and knew the doctor had gone for a time. I almost feared to open my eyes for I thought I must be dreaming but when I did at last venture a look, there she was perched on a stool close beside me, a broad grin on her face. I tried to smile but made a poor job of it.

"You've been fighting again, Mr. Duncan," she said accusingly.

I nodded but said nothing for there was nothing to be said.

"Someday you're going to get killed in a scrap," she said warningly. "Do you know that you came near dying today?"

"I have come near it many times," I said wearily. "Had I died today, there would have been no one to care. That's why I live." I stopped before the look in her eyes. I had not been asking for pity or sympathy even tho it may have sounded like it but she assuredly did not give it.

"That's a whopper," she remarked casually, "I know three people at least who would have been sorry if you had died."

"Who?"

"Captain Harrison, for one. Douglas Steele, for another and—"

"and—?" I prompted, eagerly.

"and myself," she finished.

"Little lady," I questioned softly, "would you have really cared?"

"I would," she answered looking into my eyes, "for I like you, Billy Duncan."

"And I—" The hot words were surging up to my lips but I forced them back. It would bring her no joy and perhaps cause her sorrow to know that a rough, hardened Soldier of Fortune loved her with all the force of his being and would have gone to hell and back for her. "I thank you," I finished.

"You're welcome," she answered.

There was an uncomfortable pause and then I questioned, "How goes missionarying?"

Her face took on an aggrieved expression but the corners of her mouth twitched, "Why, I think I'm getting on fine, I've started a school, you know, for the little kids. But Douglas," she frowned, "he wants me to go home. He says——," she stopped short.

"What does he say?" I questioned my interest arising.

"Oh! Nothing! It wouldn't interest you!"

"I rather think it would, please, little lady," I said eyeing her keenly.

"Well," she said defiantly, "it's Juan Mardo." She cast a lightning glance at me but my face was expressionless, "Douglas says he don't like the way he's acting, but I don't see that he's been doing anything wrong. I don't like him—I couldn't after that affair on the boat—but he's interesting and he has helped me a lot."

"Helped you?" I questioned, trying to keep an expression from my voice. She looked at me curiously and nodded.

"At first I couldn't get any of those little Japs or Chinks to come to me. I tried awfully hard, but it wasn't any use, their parents wouldn't let them. Then along came Juan Mardo and said he could bring them and he did—I've more kids than I can manage. Yet Doug kicks something awful."

"I don't blame him," I said quietly, "and I'm going to tell you something I overheard only a short time ago. Three of our crew were leaning against the rail talking, I understand Jap, all right, and they were talking about Juan Mardo and—you."

"Who? Me?" she cried in amazement, "Go on, this is getting exciting!"

"They were saying," I went on watching her to see the effect of my words, "that Juan Mardo had his eye on you—and intended to have you—any way he could get you!"

Her eyes had widened as I had been speaking and I knew she was intensely interested. "Ye Gods!" she gasped and then her grin flashed, "This is thrilling!"

"Little lady," I said, "maybe you don't know what that means."

Her eyes narrowed as she threw me a quick glance, "Ah! but I do. I'm not that unsophisticated." Then her eyes wandered to the bandage about my head and her teeth gleamed in a grin again, "That was what you fought about?"

I stared angrily for I had not intended that she should know.

But she was quick and she saw the truth, "There are mighty few men who would fight so for a woman—and I wish I could repay you—I thank you." And she put out her hand.

"You have repaid me," I said rather roughly, I fear, and I took her hand.

"You're welcome."

She went after that and I soon fell asleep my head throbbing like a ship's engine.

When I awoke, it must have been midnight or thereabouts and the moonlight was slanting in thru the glassless window. The little shack was stifling and my head was hot and aching. Getting up, I fished a box of matches from my pocket and lit one, determined to find some water. There was a candle end on the table, so I lit it and reached for the bucket of water that someone (the doctor, no doubt) had put on the floor near the bed. I had just tilted it up when I heard a few hasty steps outside, a pause and then a hesitant knock. I put down the bucket quietly and reached for my knife, for there was no one I knew who would pay me a visit at this unearthly hour.

"Who's there?" I demanded.

"Me," came a low reply.

The door flew open and there stood my little lady! She was clad in a thin white nightdress with a pink silk kimono thrown over it and as she stood there she nervously gathered it closer about her throat. Her yellow hair was loose and rumpled and her little bare feet stuck into pink silk slippers. Her lips were parted slightly for she was breathing quickly and her eyes shown like stars as she came toward me.

"My God!" I gasped and leaped forward. What was she doing here at this time, so dressed? "Go back," I cried softly, "God! Little lady, you can't come in here!"

"It'll be just as bad if I stand in the street," she

answered, softly, "Besides, I've got to see you. Mr. Duncan—I've come for the help you promised me!"

"You are in trouble?" I questioned, a choking feeling in my throat as I realized it was to <u>me</u> she had turned for aid.

"Yes—and Douglas."

I started at his name and then as my eyes ran over the little figure in the clinging pink garment, a deadly chill came into my heart for I knew that her life hereafter would be hell if anyone had seen her.

"Little lady, won't it keep—till tomorrow?"

"I know what you must think of me," she cried softly, "but this is—is life and death."

"Go on," I said briefly, seeing that something was indeed afoot.

"Well—Douglas is out gunning for Juan Mardo."

"What?" I cried, in astonishment.

"Yes," she worried on, "he got his pistol this afternoon—and he's been gone ever since—Oh! Billy Duncan, this has been an afternoon of agony! I went to bed—and then—about 5 minutes ago, I heard someone run down the street toward the docks and it was Juan Mardo."

"Go on."

"Right after him came Doug—I was at the
window and I called quietly to him—didn't you
hear me?"

I shook my head, "I was asleep. Go on."

"Doug didn't stop—I knew you would help
me so I came here."

"Go on."

"That's all."

"But it isn't all," I said quietly, a slow rage
beginning to smoulder in me against the little half
breed, "You haven't told all."

"But I have," she replied, twisting her hands
nervously.

"Not all. Why is Steele out to kill Mardo?"

She seemed to turn pale, "Doug—because—
he's—oh! because he's always hated him!"

"Yes," I said, determined to have the truth,
"Tell me little lady."

"That's the reason."

As I looked at her keenly, there rose in my
mind some of the tales of the fiendish doings of

that half breed and a terrible idea took form and sprung into life in my brain.

"What has Juan Mardo done to you?" I shot at her. She looked up into my eyes and a dull red flush crept up from neck to hair.

"Nothing—I swear," she cried frantically.

I sprang at her and caught her hands, "Tell me," I said authoritatively.

"You are hurting my hands!"

"Tell me."

"I was going into the house this afternoon," she whispered, her words tumbling over each other, "when he came up. He began to talk queerly. I tried to go in—he said—" she stopped short and tugged at her braids, "Let me go."

"Tell me."

"I can not—I will not tell you!"

"Little lady—was it—that?" Her eyes rose quickly to mine, read their meaning and she bowed her head. "God! And you—?"

"I was stunned—he tried to kiss me . . . — Stop! You're hurting my hand!—and Doug came from the house—he'd heard it all—Juan Mardo

ran, and Doug got his gun—I tried to stop him—
but he went."

"And you want me to—?"

"To stop Doug!"

"Stop him—help him you mean!"

"No! No!" she cried vehemently, "I won't have
Mardo's blood on Doug's hands because of me.
You must stop him—for my sake, Mr. Duncan!"

"Perhaps," I said and then put the question
that lay near my heart. "Little lady, you intend to
marry Douglas Steele sometime?"

A ghost of her grin crept onto her lips as she
answered, "Perhaps—why?"

"Because," I answered slowly, "he must come
to you with clean hands."

"You'll stop him, then?" she cried joyfully.

"Yes—Juan Mardo's blood must not be on his
hands," and I released her.

She walked to the door and then turned, tears
in her eyes, "God bless, Billy Duncan."

"Wait a minute," I said stepping over to her, "I
have something to show you," and I pulled my knife
from its sheath at my back and held it out to her.

It was a beautiful little dagger of Spanish steel
with a silver grip and her eyes brightened as she
took it. She peered at the haft in the uncertain
light and read the words engraved on it.

"Amigo mio," she said, aloud. "That's Spanish?"

"Yes, 'Friend O' Mine,' and it <u>has</u> been my
friend, my friends are your friends. Keep it, little
lady."

"For me?" Her eyes sparkled.

"Yes," I said grimly, "I'm afraid you'll need it
sometime—you'd better go now."

"I guess I had. Good bye, Billy Duncan," and
she held out her hand the one with the knife in it.

It was not meant for shaking so I bent and
kissed the little white hand. As my lips touched it
my eyes were near "Amigo Mio" and I breathed an
inward prayer that it would prove her friend when
she needed it. She withdrew her hand and for an
instant, stood in the door, her eyes dark wells of
light, and she was gone.

c h a p t e r
f o u r

One night, a week later, Captain Harrison stood uneasily eyeing the falling barometer. I was at the wheel at the time and I could hear him muttering something about the big storm that was coming our way. The night was stifling, there was not the slightest breeze and our empty sails sagged mournfully. The sea was glassy and we were truly "as silent as a painted ship, upon a painted ocean."

How black and still that night was! So different from a moonlight night a week ago when the little lady had come to me for aid. I did my best, that night, to justify the trust she had placed in me and tho I fulfilled her trust, my self appointed task was not a success. Ten minutes after my little lady left me, I found Douglas Steele on the waterfront, hunting for the half-breed among the bales and boxes on the wharf. I came on him suddenly as I rounded a large box and found his pistol shoved into my stomach. I was not surprised, I had rather expected such a meeting, but I was not prepared for the man I met.

Instead of the half-hysterical boy I expected, it was a grim-faced, cool headed man who confronted me. He did not try to conceal his disappointment that I was not the man for whom he was seeking but cursed softly. And there on the wharf with the murky water lapping beneath us, I told him of the little lady's words.

He looked at me curiously for a moment and then questioned quietly, "Duncan, if you loved Miss Ross would you let this fiend run rampant?"

"I don't intend to let him," I said, "I am going

to kill him, myself."

"Beg pardon, but he is my game," observed Steele, coolly.

"Steele, listen to me," I said, hardly knowing how to express myself, "You are the little lady's kind and someday—you'll—marry her." He flashed a quick glance at me but said nothing. I went on, "Steele, you can't go to her with any man's blood on your hands, no matter what a beast the man may be. Besides she wouldn't ever forget it."

"Be that as it may," he said, clipping his words off short, "I'm going to kill him."

"You mean I am," I replied.

Well, we argued there in the moonlight for half an hour and I finally got him to agree to my plan, but heaven knows reluctantly enough! He gave me his pistol and I promised that if I did not succeed that night, I would leave the gun under a big box for the "Caliban" was coming in for me at 5 o'clock. At last we shook hands and he sprinted up the crooked street, a perfect young animal, with the best of life before him.

For the rest of the night, I searched the water

front and its neighborhood but I found no Juan Mardo. So when in the early sunrise, the "Caliban" slipped up to the wharf, I shoved the pistol under the box and climbed on board with many a backward look to Senora Castro's little house.

I felt in my hip pocket for the heavy automatic I had bought at Yindano for I was going to Laysen well prepared. Then the Cap hurried up.

"Bill, something fierce is going to break loose soon."

"Typhoon, I guess," I said, carelessly, for I was thinking of other things.

"I think not. I never saw anything like this before. We've got to make for port."

"Laysen is nearest," I said. "With a fair wind we could make it in three hours."

"Only there isn't any wind," growled the Cap. "Turn in, Bill, and get some sleep. Give the wheel to Sung Lo. You'll be needed more later on."

I turned the wheel over to the Chink and went below. How long I slept, I don't know but when I awoke, the ship was pitching fearfully. A smell of sulphur was in the air and one of the crew was

pounding on my door. When I climbed on deck, a
cloud of hot ashes enveloped and almost smoth-
ered me. I made my way to where Captain Jim
stood at the wheel. He was gripping it with all his
strength, trying to keep the "Caliban" from being
swamped in the mountainous seas. As I reached his
side, a rain of burning cinders swept over us and
the Cap staggered back.

"Take the wheel, Bill," he shouted thru the up-
roar, "and keep her straight. I'll tend to the men."

"What is it?" I gasped, clinging to the wheel
of the bucking ship.

"Volcano—somewhere," came to me and then
he was gone. I let go the wheel for a moment to tie
my handkerchief over my nose and then I clung
for dear life.

All over the deck, sea birds were falling, some
dead, many flapping and squawking, all adding
more noise and confusion to the inferno. Hot
ashes and burning cinders rained down continu-
ously burning through my shirt and blistering my
skin. The light over the compass was smashed but
not before I saw the compass needle spinning

madly around. Faintly thru this war of the waters
and the confusion, I could hear Captain Jim bel-
lowing orders and the terrified screams of the
crew. Then clouds of gas rolled over us and I
began to choke but I did not release the wheel.
The "Caliban" rose to the crest of waves, how
high I could not see and with sickening lurches
shot down into the froth of them. Flood after
flood swept our decks and I remember that the
water was hot. More bursts of cinders and I was
nearly gone when the Cap reeled up.

"Lash the wheel and go below!" he ordered
hoarsely and in a half dazed way I obeyed, he
helping me.

Having done our best, we fought our way to
the companionway and went below, closing the
hatches behind us. There among the smelling,
cowering, whimpering crew I fell exhausted and
soon went to sleep.

When Captain Jim awoke me it was morning.
The sun was blazing down, not a breath of air was
blowing and the quiet sea was covered with an oily
grey ash surface. There was no wind to fill our

sails, so there we lay, becalmed, for hours. I have never known a hotter day than that one. The sun was blistering and the planks of the deck felt like a hot stove. Even the Chinks and Japs who were used to the heat, suffered that day and Captain Jim and I fairly dripped perspiration.

I know both of us would have been down with the heat had it not been for the ice we had laid in at Yindano. Along about sunset a brisk breeze came up and we headed for Laysen. The storm had driven us a good way from our track but if the breeze held we would make port at midnight. The breeze did hold and it was with an easy mind that I slept that night. Tomorrow I should see my little lady. I was having beautiful dreams when a rough hand woke me and the Cap stood beside me, pale for all his browness and I knew something was radically wrong.

"Bill, what latitude is Laysen?" And I noticed pencil and paper in his hand. I told him.

"I knew what it was—but I thought I was dreaming."

"What's up?"

"Bill, do you know that we're in that spot now?"

"No," I answered beginning to be puzzled, "Is it 12 o'clock? We were to be at Laysen then."

"Don't you understand? We are there now— but Laysen isn't!"

It took fully a minute for the hideous meaning of his words to sink in. Somehow, I was stymied, incapable of thought, and I stood staring at him.

"No—you are joking!" I managed to say, finally, but I knew before he spoke that he was not. He seemed ten years older, whiter, haggard and broken.

"I took a shot at the sun at noon," he said in a dead tone, "and worked it out. We are directly over Laysen now."

"God! Then—?"

"Laysen went down in the storm," and he looked into my eyes. Then like a thunderclap, the full significance of his last words burst on me. My mind whirled, incapable of taking it all in. I stared mutely at him and saw the same realization in his eyes. The little lady!

"It may not be," faltered Captain Jim.

"Sung Lo has steered off his course," I cried, catching at a small hope as a drowning man at the proverbial straw.

"I have been steering," he replied drearily. "Come on deck, Bill."

———— ⇒◎⇐ ————

Don't ask me about that night or the next day either. I lived as in a daze, unable to comprehend what had happened. Captain Jim cruised about all the morning but I could do nothing but think of my little lady. As I had last seen her, framed against the doorway, the light breeze whipping the pink garment about her, her eyes deep and unreadable and "Amigo Mio" held to her breast never to see her again? Never to hear the ring of her boyish laughter or to see the rollicking devil in her eye? Never again to feel the sweet womanliness of her presence? Never—never?

At noon, the Cap took another shot at the blazing sun and verified our position. There could be no mistake. Laysen was gone. The sea had swallowed it up and left no traces.

We cruised about till the afternoon, hoping

against hope that the whole thing was a hideous nightmare or that in some way we had made a monstrous mistake. But at last we turned for Yindano to bear back the sad news. It was near sunset when a cry from the steersman brought me on deck from my cabin.

"Boat ahoy!"

"Bill," came the Cap's yell full of an indescribable joy. "Bill, come up! You damned son-of-a-gun! There's the white boat!"

I came quicker than I have ever come to any man's call. I did not know what he meant but only one thing could put that note in his voice. All the crew was lined up on the starboard rail, excitedly jabbering and hopping about. Throwing several out of the way, I reached Captain Jim's side and my eyes sought what his shaking finger pointed out. The sun was setting in flaming splendor and the red tints in the west gave promise of another burning day. Across the waters was a bloody path and in the center of it, coming towards us with all sails set, was a little white boat. As it came, riding gaily over the tops of the waves and gently rising and falling in the swells, a strange silence fell on the gibbering crew.

Captain Jim bellowed across the intervening water. "Ahoy, the sailboat!"

We waited breathless for the answering hail but there was none. On came the little boat, her sails bellying in the wind and I recognized it as the one I had seen the little lady on a month before.

"Ahoy there! Why don't you answer?" yelled the Cap angrily and waited, expectantly. But with a dreary sinking of my heart, I knew that there would never be an answering call from that little white ship.

"Bill, look," whispered Captain Jim as it came nearer, "Theres—theres something lying on the deck. It's a man."

"Two men, I'm thinking," I said.

"No—three," he corrected huskily.

All at once the crew broke loose again in their ear splitting gibbering and the Cap whispered to me in a subdued voice, "Lower a boat, Bill."

I had a boat put over the side and the Cap and I and four Japs rowed over to the "Merry Maid," for that was the name on the bow. The two of us got on the little deck of the boat and walked to the first body. It was a Jap, somewhat slashed with a knife but evidently dead from a bullet in his chest. The Cap and I said nothing but looked into each other's eyes and moved to the next body. We turned him over and found that it was a big Kanaka, a scoundrelly fellow, one of Juan Mardo's satellites. He too had died of a bullet wound but he was terribly bruised and beaten about the face.

"I wonder—" whispered the Cap. The third body lay near the cracked and empty water beaker and before the Cap turned it over, I knew who it was.

"Juan Mardo," he said grimly as he examined him, "one cut on the shoulder. Lord, Bill—I'd hate to die of thirst!"

"He wasn't shot?"

"Nope. Only a little bruised. There's been a big fight somewhere. He died of thirst in that inferno, yesterday. Wasn't an easy death by his looks."

"Evidently," was all I said, but as I looked at the contorted face, I almost felt a twinge of pity for him.

Dying of thirst in the tropics is a dog's death. We turned him on his face again and it was not till then that I noticed a broad half-obliterated trail of blood that lay across the deck and into the little cubbyhole of a cabin.

"Bill," Captain Jim's voice was husky—"the cabin."

"Yes," I replied dully, for it seemed as if I were moving in a dream.

We both hung back, longing to know the worst, yet dreading what the cabin contained. But, finally I went down the three little steps, in the bloody path and into the cabin, Captain Jim close behind me. The red sunlight slanted thru the portholes and lit up the little cabin with a dreary light but the quick change from light to semi-darkness half-blinded me.

The first thing I saw was a pair of bare feet, covered with dirt and burns and lacerated by contact with sharp rocks.

"Douglas Steele," whispered Captain Jim hoarsely.

And it was. I could see well then, the sun was sinking lower and the light was better. He lay on his back, in the center of a dried pool of blood, wearing only a pair of scorched and blackened pajama trousers: all over his bare chest were knife wounds—long slashes, reaching from shoulder to waist, small deep stabs and short jagged hacks. It was Douglas Steele that I saw first. I took him in at a glance and then—

"Buck up, Bill," I heard the Cap's quivering voice in my ear—then I saw my little lady.

She sat with her back against the wall, holding Douglas Steele's head in her lap. Her eyes were closed. She was still but a quiet indescribable smile rested on her lips—the smile of a conquerer. She was dressed as I had seen her last. God knows centuries ago—in a white nightgown and the pink silk kimono.

As one in a dream, I saw Captain Jim tiptoe across the cabin to her and gently take hold of the pink silk garment.

"Bill," he whispered softly and I too, crossed the intervening space. "Look, Bill" and he drew

back the kimono. There the sun's last rays glisten-
ing on it, buried to the hilt in her white breast was
"Amigo Mio."

I remember that even in that dark hour, a
thrill of pride came over me when I realized that
it had been her friend when she needed it. There
had been but little blood, the knife itself stopped
the flow. As the sun sank below the horizon, a red
beam shot into the cabin full on her face, sending
a flush of color into her white cheeks—her smile
seemed to flash as of old—and the sun sank.

I never knew what happened next. Something
within seemed to snap. After a time, as from afar
off, Captain Jim's voice came to me.

"He carried her thru all that hell of lava and
hot ashes—he was a man—that boy! They must
have boarded this catboat—and in the smoke and
inferno, Mardo and his Japs got on too. God in
heaven, Bill, but there must have been a fight when
the storm died. No doubt the boy threw several
overboard! There's his gun."

He bent and picked up a pistol that lay near
the dead man's hand. "Empty," he said quietly as

he broke it. "He put her in the cabin and fought those fiends outside till their knives got him. He must have crawled bleeding in here to her with his empty pistol and died in her arms. And then," Captain Jim looked gravely into my eyes, "The little lady heard Juan Mardo coming—and Bill— she used 'Amigo Mio.' God bless her brave little heart—she wasn't afraid to die!"

I sat still in the gloom. For me, the bottom had fallen out of everything. There was nothing left to live for. Life was dreary, empty. The sun had left my sky and all was dark.

"Come, Bill," said the Cap gently, "we'd better go now." I rose wearily and followed him. At the door I turned and saw Douglas Steele's long body dimly outlined in the twilight. Something rose in my throat and choked me.

"Thank you, Steele," I said softly as if he had been alive, "Thank you."

"Thank you," echoed Captain Jim.

In the ever deepening twilight, Captain Jim and I stood bareheaded at the rail and watched the "Merry Maid" slowly sink. We had carried the bodies of Juan Mardo and his men in the cabin, battened down the hatches and then had stove a hole below the water line. As the twilight thickened, it sank more quickly and with it sank my heart, my hopes, my life.

Somewhere in the South Pacific lies a little white boat with a queer crew—an arch-fiend and his two imps, a man who was a <u>man</u>—and a woman who placed her honor far—far higher than her life.

F I N I S
(evidently)

———————— ∞ ————————

THE PUBLICATION OF <u>LOST LAYSEN</u> AND THE COROLLARY
LETTERS AND PHOTOGRAPHS WAS A JOINT DECISION
MADE BY THE MITCHELL ESTATE, THE FAMILY OF HENRY
LOVE ANGEL, AND THE ROAD TO TARA MUSEUM IN
response to overwhelming public interest from around the world.
Careful consideration was given to what Margaret Mitchell would have
wanted. On behalf of historians, scholars, and Mitchell fans—a
thank-you goes to them all for preserving this piece of history and the
memory of this great author.

It may be hard to imagine what Margaret Mitchell's world was like
three-quarters of a century ago. We can learn names and dates, but
realizing what prevailing views were and how they came to be is far
harder. Today we can agree on the inappropriateness of certain words
and characterizations; however, as much as Mitchell was a woman
ahead of her time, she was also very much a part of it. Margaret
Mitchell mixed her knowledge of the real world into her fiction, creating characters who spoke with the language of their era, a time when
most rough seafaring men spoke disparagingly of other races and
respected virtuous women who believed honor more sacred than life.
And, while *Gone With the Wind* raises issues from a period in American
history that is familiar to most readers, the American public's attitudes
toward the Far East in the first few decades of this century may not
leap so easily to mind. By 1916, World War I had begun in Europe. In
the United States, patriotism burned with a new glow, but with it big-
otry spread. Immigration laws were passed, and voices in the American
press began to herald the "yellow peril." Americans feared Japanese

imperialism in the Pacific, even though Japan was merely emulating the same decades-old practice by Western powers who had been busy pursuing their own "manifest destiny."

All the text in this novella and her letters appear as Margaret Mitchell scrawled in her hand more than three-quarters of a century ago. Margaret Mitchell wrote her novella and many of her letters in pencil, composing entirely in longhand. Margaret's cursive writing is difficult to read. Some punctuation or words appear almost illegible. In some sections her periods and commas appear to be the same or are missing entirely. In transcribing Margaret Mitchell's handwritten text for *Lost Laysen,* changes were not made to the original material except as indicated by brackets or for clarity; some punctuation has been added or deleted, which in some instances has resulted in capitalizing a word or redefining the beginning of a paragraph.

Extraneous writing appears on various pages of the composition books and on their covers. This writing is unrelated to the story and has been omitted. It's worth noting, though, that the word "Pledge" appears on the front cover of the first composition book, and that Mitchell shows a subtitle on both covers that reads *The Little Lady Unafraid.* On an inside page, she lists the titles of other stories, now presumably destroyed: *Man Who Never Had a Chance, Fortunes of the Four, Silver Spurs*—or *Comrades Three,* and *The Lady-Doc.*

The photographs that appear in this book may have been cropped. They may be viewed in their original state at the Road to Tara Museum. It is also worth noting that not all of the museum's collection of Angel's fifty-seven photographs appear in this book. Some images were not included because they differ only slightly from images that have been included in the book, others are out of focus, and others are damaged or otherwise difficult to make out.

B I B L I O G R A P H Y

ARCHIVAL SOURCES

Atlanta Historical Society
Emory University Special Collections
Fulton County Vital Records
Gwinnett County Historical Society
University of Georgia Libraries
Hargrett Library, Mitchell Marsh Collection

BOOKS

Atlanta City Directories, 1912–23, 1940–45.

Bryant, James C. *Capital City Club: The First One Hundred Years 1883–1983*. Atlanta: Capital City Club, 1991.

Compton's Interactive Encyclopedia. Version 3.00. Compton's Learning Company, 1994.

Edwards, Anne. *Road to Tara*. New Haven and New York: Ticknor & Fields, 1983.

Facts and Fancies. Washington Seminary School, Atlanta, Georgia, Annuals 1916, 1917, 1918.

Farr, Finis. *Margaret Mitchell of Atlanta*. New York: William Morrow, 1965.

Garrett, Franklin M. *Atlanta and Environs*. 3 vols. New York: Lewis Publishing, 1954.

―――. *Yesterday's Atlanta*. Miami: E. A. Seemann, 1974.

Grattan, C. Hartley. *The Southwest Pacific Since 1900*. Ann Arbor: University of Michigan Press, 1963.

Gwinn, Yolande. *I Remember Margaret Mitchell*. Lakemont: Copple House Books, 1987.

Harwell, Richard. *Margaret Mitchell's "Gone With the Wind" Letters, 1936–1949*. New York: Macmillan and London: Collier Macmillan Publishers, 1976.

Langsam, Walter C. *The World Since 1914*. New York: Macmillan Company, 1935.

Peacock, Jane Bonner. *A Dynamo Going to Waste—Letters to Allen Edee 1919–1921*. Atlanta: Peachtree Publishers, 1985.

Pyron, Darden Asbury. *Southern Daughter: The Life of Margaret Mitchell*. New York: Oxford University Press, 1991.

Runkle, Scott F. *An Introduction to Japanese History*. Japan: International Society for Educational Information Press, 1976.

Shavin, Norman. *Days in the Life of Atlanta*. Atlanta: Capricorn, 1987.

Shavin, Norman and Sharter, Martin. *The Million Dollar Legends: Margaret Mitchell and* Gone With the Wind. Atlanta: Capricorn, 1974.

This Fabulous Century, 1910–1920. Virginia: Time-Life Books, 1985.

Walker, Marianne. *Margaret Mitchell & John Marsh: The Love Story Behind* Gone With the Wind. Atlanta: Peachtree Publishers, 1993.

INTERVIEWS

Angel Jr., Henry. Georgia, 1994, 1995.

Britton, Sarita Hiscox. Florida, 1995.

McFadyen, Courtenay Ross. Pennsylvania (previously recorded 1980 audio by Peacock & Wiggins), 1995.

Reeves, Dorothy. Georgia, 1995.

Summers, Jessie. Georgia, 1995.
Wiggins, Patsy. Georgia, 1994, 1995.

MAGAZINES AND JOURNALS

Edwards, Augusta Dearborn, "My Most Unforgettable Character." *Reader's Digest*, March 1962, pp. 117–21.

Freer, Debra. "Margaret Mitchell Has Not Gone With the Wind." *Art & Antiques*, May 1995, pp. 54–63.

Harwell, Richard Barksdale. "A Striking Resemblance to a Masterpiece—*Gone With the Wind* in 1936." *Atlanta Historical Journal* 25 (Summer 1982): 21–38.

Howland, William S. "Peggy Mitchell, Newspaperman." *Atlanta Historical Bulletin* 9 (May 1950): 47–64.

Key, William. "Margaret Mitchell and Her Last Days on Earth." *Atlanta Historical Bulletin* 9 (May 1950): 108–27.

McKay, Blyth. "Margaret Mitchell in Person, and Her Warmth of Friendship." *Atlanta Historical Bulletin* 9 (May 1950): 100–107.

Macmillan Publishing Company. "Margaret Mitchell and Her Novel, *Gone With the Wind*" Macmillan Company Booklet, 1936.

Margaret Mitchell of Atlanta. Atlanta Public Library memorial publication, 1954.

Marsh, John R. "Margaret Mitchell and the Wide, Wide World." *Atlanta Historical* (May 1950): 32–44.

Mitchell, Stephens. "Her Brother Remembers—Margaret Mitchell's Childhood." *The Atlanta Journal Magazine Margaret Mitchell Memorial Issue.* December 1949.

———. "Margaret Mitchell and Her People in the Atlanta Area." *Atlanta Historical Bulletin* 9 (May 1950): 5–26.

Perkenson, Medora Field. "Was Margaret Mitchell Writing Another Book?" *The Atlanta Journal Magazine Margaret Mitchell Memorial Issue.* December 1949.

Pyron, Darden. "Making History: *Gone With the Wind*, A Bibliographical Essay." *Atlanta Historical Bulletin* 4 (Winter 1985–86).

Taylor, A. Elizabeth. "Women Suffrage Activities in Atlanta." *Atlanta Historical Journal* 23 (Winter 1979): 45–54.

NEWSPAPERS

Atlanta Journal and Constitution, 1915–1922.
Atlanta Journal and Constitution, March 15, 1949
Atlanta Journal and Constitution Magazine, May 16, 1954.

UNPUBLISHED MANUSCRIPTS

Wilkins, Barratt. "Victor Lamar Smith, Shadowbrook, and the Summer of 1920."

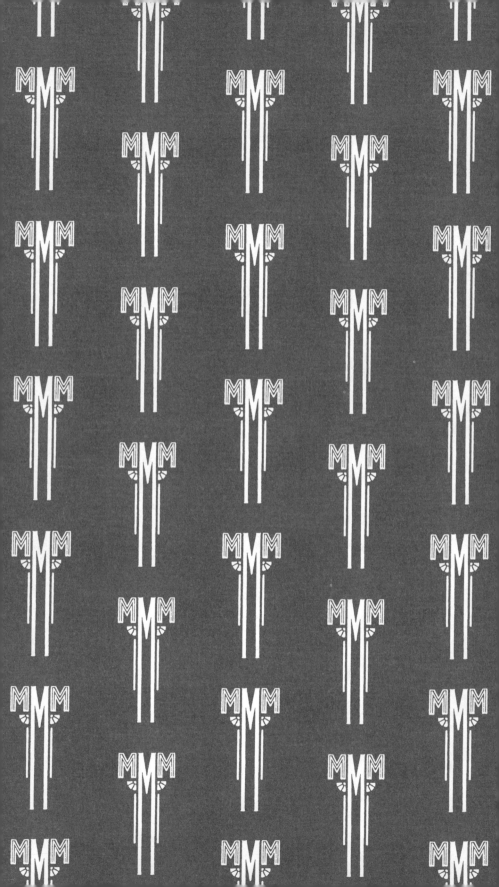